Demonic

Demonic

SHERI WHITEFEATHER

HEAT | NEW YORK

THE BERKLEY PUBLISHING GROUP
Published by the Penguin Group
Penguin Group (USA) Inc.
375 Hudson Street, New York, New York 10014, USA
Penguin Group (Canada), 90 Eglinton Avenue East, Suite 700, Toronto, Ontario M4P 2Y3, Canada
(a division of Pearson Penguin Canada Inc.)
Penguin Books Ltd., 80 Strand, London WC2R 0RL, England
Penguin Group Ireland, 25 St. Stephen's Green, Dublin 2, Ireland (a division of Penguin Books Ltd.)
Penguin Group (Australia), 250 Camberwell Road, Camberwell, Victoria 3124, Australia
(a division of Pearson Australia Group Pty. Ltd.)
Penguin Books India Pvt. Ltd., 11 Community Centre, Panchsheel Park, New Delhi—110 017, India
Penguin Group (NZ), 67 Apollo Drive, Rosedale, Auckland 0632, New Zealand
(a division of Pearson New Zealand Ltd.)
Penguin Books (South Africa) (Pty.) Ltd., 24 Sturdee Avenue, Rosebank, Johannesburg 2196,
South Africa

Penguin Books Ltd., Registered Offices: 80 Strand, London WC2R 0RL, England

This book is an original publication of The Berkley Publishing Group.

This is a work of fiction. Names, characters, places, and incidents either are the product of the author's imagination or are used fictitiously, and any resemblance to actual persons, living or dead, business establishments, events, or locales is entirely coincidental. The publisher does not have any control over and does not assume any responsibility for author or third-party websites or their content.

PRINTING HISTORY
Heat trade paperback edition / August 2011

Library of Congress Cataloging-in-Publication Data

Whitefeather, Sheri.
Demonic / Sheri Whitefeather.—Heat trade paperback ed.
    p. cm.
 ISBN 978-0-425-24141-7
 1. Demonology—Fiction. I. Title.
 PS3623.H5798D46 2011
 813'.6—dc22
                                    2010054382

PRINTED IN THE UNITED STATES OF AMERICA

10 9 8 7 6 5 4 3 2 1

One

An exclusive sex club where people either dressed up as super-natural beings or donned their best groupie gear . . .

Aeonian was a bizarre place, or so Jane Brooks had heard. But that was the point, wasn't it? To go there and evaluate the hot and dirty weirdness? In her line of work it was called research. Jane was writing a piece for *L.A. Underground*, a publication that featured the spicy and often seedy sides of the city.

She stood in front of the gilded mirror in her garage-sale-gone-wild bedroom and smoothed her little shimmy of a dress. Beneath the silky taupe fabric, which plunged lusciously low in front, she was braless. Jane had never grown out of an A cup, leaving her lacking in the cleavage department, but at least she possessed perky nipples.

She glanced at the bedside clock. Her best gal pals, Emily Torres and Suzanne Quinn, were in the living room waiting for her. Jane was rarely ready on time. But they expected as much.

Returning to her primping, she studied her reflection. She'd pinned her auburn hair into a tousled twist and painted her lips a glossy cinnamon hue.

With a critical eye, she slipped on a pair of heels the same color of her skin, then went into the living room.

Her friends sat on the couch. In tandem, they stood up.

"You look amazing," Suzanne said.

"Thank you." Jane more than appreciated the compliment. Suzanne knew her stuff. She was an up-and-coming fashion designer.

Tonight tall, blonde Suzanne was swathed in a candy-pink mini and a glorious tan. The shiny metal straps on the dress were made of big gold loops, and the formfitting, front-wrap bodice combined with a push-up bra gave her medium-sized boobs a boost.

Jane turned toward Emily. She was a properly behaved history teacher who was shy about showing off her assets. Although she had long dark locks and the curves of a Latina goddess, she'd done nothing to maximize the effect. A pastel headband kept her glorious hair from falling forward, and she wore a pair of jeans and a summer-print blouse, all buttoned up.

Jane said, "You realize that we're going to a sex club, right? And we're supposed to look like groupies?"

Emily responded, "Of course I know where we're going, and I never should've let you two talk me into it."

Suzanne chimed in. "It'll be fun. Besides, we're not going to participate. We're just going to watch." She waggled her eyebrows. "Like voyeurs."

The brunette's cheeks flushed. "I suppose I am a little curious about what sort of things they do there."

Jane shot Suzanne a conspiratorial smile. They'd been trying to loosen up Emily for years. Or at least bring her out of her good-girl shell.

Tackling the wardrobe dilemma, Suzanne unbuttoned Emily's blouse, where her bountiful breasts spilled out from a beige lace bra.

"There," the designer said. "Now she looks almost as slutty as we do."

"Almost," Jane agreed.

From there, they dragged Emily into the bathroom and did a smoky number on her eyes. A coat of flaming berry lipstick followed. The headband went bye-bye and her hair was finger fluffed. After decorating her with glittering earrings, they forced her into icy blue pumps from Jane's closet. The result was sex-kitten hot. But Emily wasn't impressed. She squirmed at her wild unveiling.

"Someone is going to want to fuck me," she said.

The horrified way she spewed the f-word made Jane and Suzanne laugh.

"You'll be fine," Suzanne promised. "Right, Janiac?"

"Totally fine," she responded, as they left her apartment and climbed into her car.

Bound for decadence.

Emily sat in the backseat, fussing with the front of her blouse. She wanted to re-button it, but Jane and Suzanne would probably pitch a fit if she covered herself. She felt self-conscious dressed this way, and on top of that, her feet hurt. The shoes were a tad too tight.

The ladies who'd given her the makeover were doing just fine, laughing and talking and singing with the radio.

Silent, Emily quit tugging at her blouse. She wished she could be more like her friends. Jane was adventurous and imaginative, and Suzanne was trendy and sassy. The three of them had been college roommates, and even then, Emily knew she was the odd woman out.

Suzanne glanced over her shoulder. "You okay, Auntie Em?"

She nodded and forced a smile. Auntie Em, Janiac, and Susie Q. Their nicknames pretty much said it all.

As they traveled deep into the concrete jungle that was L.A., Suzanne went back to singing, and Emily returned to her nervous thoughts.

She didn't do well at regular clubs, let alone a place of this sort.

What kind of people pretended to be supernatural beings? And what kind of people trailed after them behaving like groupies?

Anxious, she peered out the window. They weren't in a populated part of the city. Downtown was weird that way. Some of it was isolated, particularly at night.

Finally Jane pulled up to the gate of an underground parking structure and put a keycard into the designated slot. Aeonian was a members-only establishment, and Jane had acquired the necessary guest passes, but then Janiac was clever that way.

Emily's stomach went tight. She wanted to go home and watch something safe on TV, but it was too late for that.

They parked and got out of the car. As they walked toward the elevator of the four-story industrial building that housed the club, the heels of her too-tight shoes hit the asphalt like bullets from a machine gun. The other women's shoes echoed the same rat-a-tat-tat.

"What does Aeonian mean?" Suzanne asked Jane.

The writer responded, "Everlasting. Like heaven's eternal bliss or hell's perpetual fires."

"That's wicked cool," the designer remarked.

Or just plain wicked, Emily thought. As they reached the elevator, a trio of well-statured men appeared from the other side of the parking lot.

Suzanne looked up and said, "Damn."

Jane seconded the motion with a quiet, "No shit."

Emily more than agreed. She almost expected a haze of fog to be floating around them.

None of the women pushed the elevator button. They merely stood there, gazing at the male figures. Even from a distance, Emily could see that they sported crisp white shirts, long-tailed jackets, vests, and boots.

Suzanne said, "I wonder if they're supposed to be vampires."

Jane hadn't even blinked. "They don't look all that pale to me."

Suzanne keened out a little moan. "They're coming this way."

Emily stabbed the elevator button, hoping the men didn't make it in time.

No such luck.

They arrived on the scene, greeted the women with interest, and waited for the elevator, too. Each man was handsome in his own right, and although they stood about the same height with similar builds, they didn't look alike.

Except for their eyes.

Their irises were as black as midnight. Not that any fool couldn't tell that they were wearing colored contact lenses, but the opaque shade created a haunting effect.

And to make matters worse, the pairing of partners had already begun, starting with the man on the right, who zeroed in on Jane.

That prompted the slightly dazed writer to ask, "Who are you guys?"

He responded in a sleek and sexy way. "I'm Marcus, and I'm a demon." He motioned to his companions. "They are, too. We're all immortal."

Oh, Lord. As Jane introduced herself to Marcus, Emily whispered a prayer in her mind. This game wasn't the least bit amusing. She'd been taught to fear the devil's realm.

"What is a demon, exactly?" Suzanne asked, as the guy in the middle checked her out.

Marcus answered, "There are different breeds. Our breed descends from fallen angels. People sometimes think that all demons are fallen angels, but they're not."

As Emily shifted her feet, a different man, the one on the left, fixed his sights on her. He scanned the tops of her breasts, making his attraction to her known. She wanted to button her blouse more than ever.

He lifted his gaze, and they stared at each other. Chestnut hair fell across his forehead in wavy disarray and serious features lent him the intensity of a Renaissance man.

He said to her, "I'm Damien. And who might you be?"

"Em . . . Emily," she sputtered. She wasn't comfortable with his name. The kid in *The Omen* was called Damien, and he was the offspring of Satan.

But then this Damien smiled, flashing a one-sided dimple, and she was struck by how gently handsome it made him look. Almost like an angel.

A fallen angel, she reminded herself.

"It must be stuck," he said suddenly and reached past her to tap the elevator button.

She noticed that he did it with his left hand. Centuries ago, it was believed that left-handed people were servants of the devil. Those superstitions had changed, but that did little to temper her anxiety.

She was horribly, dangerously attracted to Damien.

Finally the elevator door opened, and everyone stepped inside. Damien used his left hand again to direct them to the lobby level, which was where the entrance of the club was located.

Emily glanced expectantly at her friends, hoping they would come to her rescue, but they were deep in the throes of demon fever, too.

As the elevator jerked and made its ascent, Suzanne couldn't take her eyes off of the hottie who'd singled her out.

Like her, he was blond, and he wore his hair short and wonderfully wild. The half-spiked, half-smoothed style put him at the top of his game, and so did those mysterious eyes. She couldn't stop staring at him.

"Why haven't I ever seen you here before?" he asked in a slightly southern voice. "Are you a new member?"

She made a small sweeping motion that included Jane and Emily. "We have passes. But just for tonight."

"So, you're a guest groupie? Then I'd better not waste any time."

He moved closer, and her pulse zinged straight to her pussy. When he pressed his mouth to her ear, she inhaled the citrus-and-spice scent of his skin.

"Have you ever done anything dirty in public?" he asked.

"No." Not until now. He was toying with the hem of her dress, lifting it just enough to make her breath rush out.

"Do you want to do bad things with me?" he whispered.

God, yes. She almost gave him permission to put his hand inside her panties.

Then she heard a throat clear. Emily, no doubt, reminding her that they weren't supposed to engage in any activity tonight. But Suzanne couldn't seem to help it.

Was she crazy? Letting this strange guy with the strange eyes seduce her in front of her friends?

She met his gaze, and he smiled. Emily's throat clearing hadn't bothered him a bit. Well, of course not, she told herself, or he wouldn't be pulling this naughty stunt.

"What's your name?" she asked him.

"Jacob Keller. But I prefer Jake. And you?"

"Suzanne Quinn. Sometimes my friends call me Susie Q."

"Like the song?"

He sang a few of the lyrics into her ear, and his southern rock tone slid sensuously over her skin. Like custard spiked with moonshine.

Damn but she wanted to kiss him. Apparently he had the same urge. He turned his head so their mouths could meet.

As the kiss unfolded, he rubbed his pelvis against hers. But he did it gently, and the contrast of his strong male body, especially the hardness behind his zipper, made the kiss more erotic than it should have been. His mouth was slightly opened and so was hers, but there was no tongue.

No noise in the background, either. No shifting of feet, no deliberate throat clearings, no low-talking voices.

Was everyone else watching?

Was Auntie Em embarrassed? Was Janiac intrigued? Were the other two men turned on, their cocks nudging their trousers?

By now Jake had both hands pressed against the elevator wall, caging Suzanne with his arms. He intensified the kiss, teasing her with his bad-boy game, running his tongue along the seam of her lips. She heard herself moan. Her panties were actually getting wet.

At that creamy moment, she didn't care why this man had such an openly lewd effect on her. All that mattered was keeping him close. She put her arms around his waist, making damn sure his pelvis remained fused to hers.

Thud!

The jerky motion of the elevator coming to a stop jarred her back to reality. She let go of Jake's waist. He flashed his devil-may-care smile and lowered his arms, freeing her from his cage.

Suzanne looked at her friends. Jane had her head tilted at an entranced angle, and Emily was staring at her as if she'd just sprouted horns and a forked tail.

Gosh, she thought, maybe she had. But instead of checking to see if she had new appendages, she glanced at Jake's buddies to get their reactions.

Damien had his hungry gaze fixed on Emily, and Marcus seemed unfazed by it all. Did that mean he was into even kinkier stuff? That when he decided it was time to seduce Jane, hell would really break loose?

Everyone piled out of the elevator and stepped into a dimly lit lobby that showcased Victorian, medieval, and mystical furnishings, along with a fancy hotel-style desk.

On the other side of the Gothic-inspired room was a set of ornately carved double doors, closed tight. An imposing bouncer stood in front of them, and the hip-thrusting music that penetrated the wood was a telltale sign that the club was in full swing.

Suzanne turned her attention to the desk. Behind it was a busty blonde in a fuck-me outfit only the most experienced groupie would dare to wear. She looked up and smiled, greeting the men as if she'd had the pleasure of knowing each of them intimately. That didn't sit well with Suzanne. She was already getting territorial over Jake.

From one little elevator kiss?

She glanced over at him and caught him looking at her, too. That made her feel better, and she chastised herself for it. She didn't belong with him any more than Emily belonged with Damien or Jane with Marcus.

Yet here they were.

Jane removed the guest passes from her purse, and they presented them to the blonde in charge.

She said, "Have fun tonight, ladies." She turned and smiled at the men again. "You gentlemen take good care of them."

"We intend to," Marcus answered.

"Damn straight," Jake echoed.

"Absolutely," was Damien's reply.

And before they knew it, Suzanne and her friends were being escorted into a sex club.

Where anything could happen.

Two

The entrance to Aeonian erupted into a seventies-style disco-
theque, and Jane did her best to take it in. Strobe lights created flashing hues, and black lights illuminated anything that
contained phosphorus or fluorescent materials, including the
erotic artwork on the walls.

Between the spinning pace of the music and the beautifully
bizarre patrons dancing, howling, and laughing, the disco was
beyond noisy. Some people were naked, some were scantily clad,
and others were fully clothed. As far as Jane could tell, no one
was having down-and-out sex in this portion of the club, but
fingers, tongues, claws, and fangs were everywhere, with lots of
phony creatures on the prowl.

Marcus was in front of her, holding her hand and dragging

her along with him. She glanced back to check on Suzanne and Emily, but she didn't see them.

She tugged on Marcus's hand, but he continued pulling her through the crowd to God only knew where. She tugged again, and he turned around.

"My friends are gone," she said above the music.

"Jake and Damien probably took them in another direction."

Well hell, she thought. She hadn't counted on being separated. "I have to find them."

Marcus's white shirt glowed under the black lights. "They'll be fine. No one is going to hurt them."

Easy for him to say. Emily was still a babe in the woods, and after that sensual elevator show, Suzanne was destined for trouble.

"Come with me, Jane. I know of a quiet corner where we can talk and get to know each other."

She should've insisted on searching for her friends, but there was something about Marcus that made her follow him.

Was it the way shadows played upon his face? Or was it his smooth yet commanding voice? Of course it could be those deliberately dark eyes.

As he led her through the crowd again, she studied the broad expanse of his back. He wore his licorice black hair in a ponytail at his nape, and although he was pretending to be immortal, he looked around thirty.

Jane had to admit that this demon thing was wildly fascinating. Should she include that in her article? The effect of falling for a so-called supernatural?

She couldn't help but wonder what he was like outside of the club. Would she still follow him blindly? Or was it the atmosphere that enhanced his appeal?

Marcus escorted her out of the disco and down a sconce-lit corridor, then steered her toward an alcove with a velvet settee and invited her to sit with him.

The misty watercolor above the settee depicted an old-fashioned blonde dressed in a shredded petticoat. Seated on a straight-back chair with her arms tied behind her back and metal clamps attached to her nipples, she still managed to look demure.

"Damien painted that," Marcus said.

Mercy, she thought, worried about Emily again. "He's into S and M?"

"No. He painted it for me."

Jane's heart hit her chest. "Is that why you brought me to this spot? To show me the kind of sex you favor?"

His erotic response was, "You could be her."

She shook her head. "My hair is a different color."

"I was speaking metaphorically."

She dared another glance at the painting. "I'm not into that sort of thing."

"Have you tried it?"

"No."

"Aren't you the least bit curious?"

Was she? To save herself from thinking too deeply about it, she revealed her agenda. "I came here to observe, not participate. I'm writing an article about the club for *L.A. Underground*."

"That's an interesting publication."

"I might include you in the article. But I won't use your name. I'll protect your identity."

"Why? In case I have a corporate job or I'm keeping my lifestyle a secret? I'm comfortable with who I am."

"So am I."

"Are you sure about that?"

Did he think she was denying herself pleasure? "My nickname is Janiac."

He arched his brows. "Does that mean you're some sort of maniac?"

"I partied a lot in college." She lifted her chin, determined not to let him intimidate her. "I've had lots of lovers, too."

"But none who chained you up? Or blindfolded you? Or made you call him sir before he pushed his cock into your mouth?"

"I'm too much of a control freak to let a man dominate me." Even if shivers were crawling up and down her spine, even if she was oddly aroused.

"I'm a hypnotist, Jane, and my practice is dedicated to erotic hypnosis. Mostly I work with couples, and releasing inhibitions and exploring fantasies are common goals among my clients." He leaned closer, his voice caressingly soft. "Women like yourself often have secret longings to relinquish control. They have repressed fantasies about becoming sexually submissive."

Holy shit. She squeezed her thighs together. "Have you been hypnotizing me? Is that why I agreed to wander off with you and leave my friends behind?"

"What you did, you did of your own free will. I had nothing to do with it."

He was wrong. He had everything to do with it. She was insanely attracted to him, and being in his proximity was making her head spin. If she had any sense, she would walk away. She would find Emily and Suzanne and get the hell out of here. But somewhere in the core of her confused soul, she wanted to stay.

Did that mean Marcus was right about her? Did she have repressed fantasies?

"Would you like to see my favorite place in the club?" he asked.

Yes, no, maybe? "Is it a BDSM dungeon of some kind?"

He nodded. "Are you game?"

"To watch, not play," she told him. "And it's strictly for research."

They stood up, and she landed eye to chest with him. Fighting the difference in their heights, she lifted her head to meet his gaze, proving, she hoped, that she was his equal.

"Are you aware of the rumors?" he asked.

"What rumors?"

"Some people at the club think that there are actually real supernaturals who frequent this place."

Good grief. "Do people think you and your friends are real demons?"

"Supposedly only one of us is real, and the other two are protecting his secret."

"That's absurd." But this was an occult-inspired environment and silly stories were bound to surface. She should have expected as much. "I don't believe in things that go bump in the night."

Marcus shrugged. "I'm just repeating the rumor."

"The sex-club gossip mill? Should I mention that in my article, too?"

"You can write whatever you want. I was just giving you a heads-up." He reached out and grasped a loose tendril of her pinned-up hair. "But for the record, I do have a demonic side in bed." Taking his declaration to the next level, he rubbed his thumbs over her nipples, which were standing at attention beneath the plunging neckline of her dress. "Especially when the submissive, the sub, is clamped good and tight and begging for more."

His touch ignited a flame, there at her breasts and lower, much lower, where she became aware of the crotch of her panties pressed against her cunt. "I'm not a sub."

"In my mind you are."

And his mind was dangerous, she thought. Anyone who could hypnotize another person was probably capable of subliminal messages in everyday talk. She leaned into his touch. Not that this conversation qualified as everyday talk.

He removed his hands from the front of her dress, leaving her nipples bereft and aching for more.

"Ready to go to the dungeon now?" he asked.

What she wanted was to lie down and spread her legs for him. "I need something to drink first." A long cool beverage to wet her mouth and keep her from licking the salt off his skin.

"There's a bar in the dungeon."

They left the alcove, and he led her down another corridor. When they came to a heavy wooden door with iron hardware and a stone gargoyle looming above it, she knew they'd arrived.

He opened the door, and she took a deep breath and crossed the threshold. The main room in the dungeon was a reception area with a rustic bar, scattered tables, and two black sofas splashed with bloodred pillows. The sofas were inhabited by groupies, and Jane got the feeling that they were lolling about, waiting for someone to choose them for a bit of torturous play.

One girl entertained herself while she waited. Sporting a rubber jumpsuit with a cutout that exposed her genitals, she moaned softly and stroked her petal pink clit.

Marcus drew Jane's attention back to him. "What would you like to drink?"

"Anything, as long as it's a mocktail."

A faint smile floated across his lips. "Janiac likes virgins? Personally they're too innocent for my blood."

She decided not to volley his remark. "I'm the designated driver tonight."

He went over to the bar and returned with a lusty lime mocktail, a simple beverage that consisted of lime, Coke, and ice.

She took a refreshing sip and glanced at the rubber-clad girl. Jane couldn't imagine touching herself in front of strangers.

"Her master makes her do that," Marcus said, then gestured to shadowed-shrouded corner of the room, where a man in a werewolf getup was watching his groupie-slave.

Was he rumored to be real, too?

Jane couldn't deny that he had his act down pretty well, with his big hairy body and glowing yellow eyes.

She turned and focused on Marcus's eyes. "Colored contacts are big around here."

"They create the desired effect." He stared back at her. "As soon as you finish your drink, I'll show you the community playroom in the dungeon."

She broke eye contact. She knew better than to look at him for too long. "Community?"

"Where anyone can go, either to participate or to watch. The individual playrooms are for private use and have to be reserved in advance."

"Have you ever booked a room?"

"Yes, but not in a while. I'm on the lookout for a new sub, someone who's never experienced this lifestyle before."

She downed the rest of her lusty lime virgin. "Don't expect me to volunteer."

"We'll see." He took her empty glass and set it on the table beside the clit-stroking groupie, who was working herself into a hot little frenzy.

Jane thought she heard the werewolf emit a low growl as the girl came, but when she glanced his way, he was silent.

Marcus reached for her hand and led her away from the reception area and down a hallway with numbered doors. The private playrooms, no doubt.

They turned a corner, and she marveled at what a maze the club was. Suzanne and Emily could be anywhere. Hell, she could be anywhere. Without Marcus, she probably wouldn't be able to find her way out of this place.

What had she been thinking, putting herself at his mercy? This was by far the dumbest thing she had ever done. Dumb, but exciting. Her heart pounded with every step.

The next corridor had medieval torture devices bolted to the walls, and a ball of heat curled low in her belly.

"Almost there," Marcus said.

Suddenly she realized how tightly she was clinging to his hand. She let go and reminded herself to breathe.

They turned another corner and came to a door similar to the one that led to the dungeon's reception area, gargoyle and all.

In the quiet, their gazes locked. Anticipation swirled through her body, and she waited for him to kiss her. But instead, he stepped back, leaving her longing for the mysterious taste of his lips. Was that part of his domination? A glimmer of what being his sub would be like?

He opened the door, and the activity in the community playroom spun before her eyes.

She knew that BDSM entailed bondage and discipline, dominance and submission, and sadism and masochism. But witnessing those acts in person . . .

"I don't know where to look," she said.

"Anywhere that pleases you," was Marcus's reply.

He placed his hand on the swell of her back and guided her farther into the playroom.

The scent of melting wax permeated the air and so did the heady smell of sex. The room was wide in some spots and long and narrow in others, mimicking a castle dungeon. The walls were brick, and things like stockades, X-framed crosses, and whipping poles were being utilized in every imaginable way. A row of prison cells had slaves locked inside.

Jane gazed at the first cell where two naked women, seated on the ground and facing each other, were bound together with rope. Their master, a gorgeous guy flashing his phony fangs, also had a raging hard-on jutting out of his leather pants.

"Do you want to see more of the cells?" Marcus asked from beside her.

She nodded, and they moved to the next one. Getting a tad braver, she inched closer to the bars.

Locked inside was a female groupie, standing upright and chained to the wall. Around her ankles was a leather-and-metal device that forced her legs apart. She wore little suction cups on her nipples that most likely created the sensation of being sucked. Her master, a dark-cloaked man playing the part of a warlock, was on his knees. He stimulated her with a "magic" vibrator and warned her not to come.

"Orgasm denial," Marcus said, his breaths tickling the nape of Jane's neck.

She hadn't realized that he'd moved forward to stand behind her. She didn't dare turn around. "What will happen if she comes?"

"He'll probably punish her."

"How?"

"With whatever means is within her limits. A sub sets the limits, the things that can and can't be done, how much of it is tolerable and for how long."

Jane had never considered her sexual limits. But she'd never been with anyone like Marcus. "I don't think I'd be good at orgasm denial."

"That's half the fun."

She did her damnedest to keep her wits. She could actually imagine being bound to his bed while he did wicked things to her.

Cripes. "I should go."

He nuzzled her shoulder. "Go where?"

The tenderness in his touch wasn't fair. "To find my friends. But I need you to walk me out. I don't want to get lost."

"I think we should stay." He slipped his arms around her waist, bringing the back of her body against the front of his. "Just a while longer."

Until the slave had an orgasm? Until the warlock punished her? Locked in Marcus's arms, Jane all but quavered.

Finding Suzanne and Emily could wait.

Three

Emily shared a table with Suzanne, Jake, and Damien, and although they'd snaked their way through the disco to an outdoor bar in the club where they could a carry on a conversation without shouting, no one had said much of anything.

Not that Suzanne and Jake cared about conversing. She was straddling his lap in a forward position, with her itty-bitty dress hiked to the very tops of her thighs while he kissed the living hell out of her.

But everything about this night was a *living hell*, Emily thought. Damien had ordered a round of green demons, a cocktail Emily had yet to touch, even though she was beyond thirsty.

As she turned her head to avoid the dirty-kissing fest, she ran smack-dab into Damien's black gaze, and his masculine beauty made her throat raw. Before Lucifer had fallen from grace, he'd been one of the most beautiful creatures in the universe.

"Try your drink," he said.

"I don't want it."

"Then I'll order you something else."

She shook her head. She didn't want anything that came from this creepy club. He reached for his drink, and she watched him take an icy sip.

She resisted the urge to wet her parched lips. "What do you think happened to Jane?"

"Marcus probably took her to the dungeon to introduce her to his lifestyle."

As a twisted image of Jane being tortured entered her mind, she clasped her hands together to keep them from trembling. "If he hurts her, I'll kill him."

"That's very noble of you, but he would never do anything to her that isn't consensual. We're not monsters, Emily."

"Then what are you?"

He took another sip of his demon cocktail, then softly said, "Men."

Bad men, she thought. She stole a glance at Jake and Suzanne and felt her cheeks go embarrassingly hot. Jake had his hand inside Suzanne's panties.

Now where was she supposed to look? Back at Damien? She realized that from his vantage point, he could see everything Jake was doing to Suzanne.

"Emily?"

Shoot. Now Damien was talking to her. She forced herself to meet his gaze. "What?"

"Go ahead and try your drink. It'll help you relax."

As much as she hated to admit it, she knew he was right. Her thirst was getting unbearable. Slowly, cautiously, she picked up the highball glass and brought the rim to her lips. The first sip of the green liquid tasted like heaven, and she cursed herself for liking it.

"Good?" he asked.

She nodded. "What's in it?"

An evening breeze rustled his wavy hair. "Nothing suspicious."

"That's not a drink recipe."

He flashed his one-dimpled smile. "Melon liqueur, rum, vodka, and lemonade."

Did he have to be so charming? She wanted to dislike him, but he was making it tough on her.

After she ate the maraschino cherry from her cocktail, his smile deepened and he asked, "Do you want mine, too?"

Coming from him that sounded sweet and sinful, but the lusty noises Suzanne was making weren't helping.

Damien lifted it from his drink. "Do you?"

He was sitting close enough to feed her, but she wasn't about to open her mouth. She took the stem from him and ate it by herself. The juicy flavor exploded on her tongue, and she wondered if it was some sort of sensual omen that his cherry tasted better than hers.

Suzanne made another excited sound, making Emily wish for the umpteenth time that she'd hadn't agreed to come to this corruptive place.

Feeling the need to apologize for her friend, she spoke in a hushed tone. "Suzanne's not usually so free in public."

Damien tilted his head. "I think she's getting ready to come."

Oh, good grief. Could things get any worse? She wanted to give Suzanne a swift kick, but that would probably only propel her tighter onto Jake's lap and cause his probing fingers to go deeper.

As a stream of "oh, Gods" and carnal gasps mingled with jerky movements, Emily pressed her knees together. The table was vibrating. And Damien, damn him, was still leaning his head to one side like the captive audience he'd become.

Finally, silence and stillness befell them.

"It's over," Damien said, punctuating the moment.

Emily cleared her lungs and braved a glance at Suzanne. The blonde had her head on Jake's shoulder, and he was holding her exceptionally close. Their afterglow actually seemed romantic until he cooed, "Let's do that again, Susie Q," and she responded with a breathy, "Okay."

Seriously? Emily grabbed her drink and downed the rest of it in two seconds flat. Damien started to laugh, and she rolled her eyes, but then she laughed, too. Jake already had his hand back in Suzanne's panties.

"They're a lost cause," she said.

"So it seems. We can go upstairs if you'd like."

"Are people doing things out in the open up there?"

"Not on the third floor, and that's where I was going to take you."

Then that certainly sounded better than staying here for the second act. "All right."

He stood up and helped her scoot back her chair, playing the perfect gentleman or the perfect immortal or whatever it was he prided himself on portraying.

They returned to the interior of the club, and he escorted her to a polished wood staircase and took her to the aforementioned third floor, which was brightly lit with a row of colorful doors.

Because they were the only club goers around, she couldn't help but ask, "What goes on in these rooms?"

"Self-expressive things." He gestured to a door with an apple painted on the outside of it. "That's the food-play center. I think they're having a pasta primavera orgy tonight."

She made a horrible face.

He raised his brows. "You don't like white sauce?"

"Not if other people's private parts are rolling around in it."

He bit back a grin, and she smacked his arm. She was starting to like him more and more.

She pointed to another door. "What happens there?"

"That's the sensation center. Feathers, vibrators, faux fur, massage oils, textured toys, whatever makes you or your partner feel good." He looked directly into her eyes. "Sometimes I play in the sensation center."

She glanced away, her heart beating much too quickly. She didn't want to think about his erotic preferences.

When they came to a red-splattered door, he said, "That's the blood bank, where vampires pretend to feed and groupies roll around in fake blood."

She wondered if some of the wannabe vamps cut other people's skin and sucked on their blood for real. She'd heard about weirdos who did things like that, and some of the clientele at this crazy place seemed way too hard core.

He continued the tour. "Over there is the art center. For body painting, cosmetic applications, henna, and airbrush tattoos. That's my favorite place in the club."

Emily didn't ask if sexual activity was encouraged during the art process. She could tell by his expression that it was. Before the energy between them became palpable, she deliberately focused elsewhere and noticed one last door.

"What's in there?"

"The museum."

"Is it a living museum for people to show off their body art?"

"No. It's a traditional museum, but with an erotic and supernatural theme. Do you want see the work that's displayed? Some of it is mine."

She turned to face him again. "You're an artist?"

He nodded. "I've donated lots of paintings to the club, but they've commissioned me for pieces, too."

She nearly sank into his black eyes. He was staring at her with anticipation. She couldn't very well say that she wasn't interested in his art, which would have been a lie anyway. She was morbidly curious about him.

"Yes, of course. I'd like to see your work."

They approached the door, and as they entered the museum, she braced herself for the themes he'd mentioned.

An instant hush fell between them. Being alone in the hallway was bad enough, but being surrounded by explicit art with no one else present created the kind of sexual tension Emily wanted to run from.

The most prominent piece was a life-sized statue of a woman exposing her wet and glistening vulva. Emily tried to glance past it, but it was darn hard to miss.

Then, drawn to the other side of the room, she wandered over to a watercolor that caught her eye. It depicted a delicate maiden in a moonlit forest with glow-in-the-dark flowers gently twining themselves around her modestly arched body.

Damien came up beside her. "That's mine."

"It's beautiful, and your talent is exceptional."

"Thank you." He gestured to another painting of the same maiden, only in this depiction the flowers were dying and looming in one of the trees was a demonic creature silently stalking her. "That's mine, too."

Heaven forbid. The creature's claws were bared, his lips were drawn into a snarl, and the head of his erect penis was shaped like the tip of a spear.

"I've been thinking about doing a third one in this series." He spoke in a penetrating tone. "But I haven't decided how the scene should play out. Do you think the maiden should tame him?"

"Is it even possible for a virgin to tame a horrible creature like that?"

"What makes you think she's a virgin?"

"She looks innocent."

"So do you."

She struggled not to squirm under his scrutiny. Between the heavy-handed makeup she was wearing, the too-tight heels, and her boobs sticking out of her blouse, she wasn't supposed to radiate innocence. "I'm supposed to look like a groupie."

"You're fetching, Emily. But you don't have the aura of a groupie." He continued to sweep his gaze over her. "Are you a virgin?"

She should have told him that it was none of his business, but she said, "No, and in my opinion sex isn't what it's cracked up to be."

"Only a woman who's never had a man give her an orgasm would say that."

She defended herself. "I've only been with a couple of men. Besides, what difference does it make if you do it to yourself or if someone does it for you? At least I can come."

"I wasn't accusing you of being frigid."

"Frigid?" Did people even say that anymore? "That's from the Victorian era."

"It's in the urban dictionary, too." He cocked his head. "And what do you know about the Victorian era?"

"I teach history at a community college."

"You barely look old enough to be out of college yourself."

Placing his hand on her spine, he led her to a window in the museum, where a view of other industrial buildings created towering shapes in the night.

He turned toward her, inspiring her to turn in his direction, too.

"I want you to come to my house," he said. "Not tonight, but another night, when you're ready to lie naked on my bed with your hair fanned on my pillow and your lovely legs spread."

Panic gripped her hard and tight, but so did an instant pulse between her thighs. "I can't. I—"

"Just think about it, Emily. Think about being with me."

He trailed a finger along her throat, stopping just shy of her cleavage. "I can make you come. I can be the first man to do that for you."

He leaned in to kiss her, and like a fool, she let it happen. As his mouth settled over hers, heat scorched her body and she melted over him like a charred marshmallow. As clichéd as it sounded, all she could think was that he had fire in his touch.

Beautiful fire. Wicked fire.

She'd never felt like this, and he was barely using his tongue. She shuddered to think how it would feel if he unleashed his full power.

She pushed against his shoulders, signaling for him to end

the connection. He did, immediately, letting her know that he wouldn't take more than she was willing to give. But that did little to ease her fear.

Because somewhere deep inside, she longed to give him everything.

Four

Suzanne sighed through the sexual haze that Jake had created. "Are you okay?" he asked.

Was she? "I think so." All she knew was that she'd been sitting on his lap, having multiple orgasms. "I've never done anything like this before."

"You look beautiful."

With her dress rolled around her hips and her panties wet? "I try."

He chuckled, then lifted her onto her own chair, where she swayed a little in her seat.

"Does this mean you're done with me?" she asked.

"No way, sweetheart. I'm just giving you a chance to catch your breath." He lifted his drink, then scowled and put it back down. "Damien and his green demons." He turned and waved a waitress over.

The scantily clad gal showed up with a smile.

"Will you bring me a Corona, sugar?" He turned to Suzanne. "Do you want a different drink, honey?"

"No. This is fine." She liked melon liqueur, but she wasn't sure if she liked the sweethearts, sugars, and honeys that Jake tossed around. But she supposed it was a southern thing.

After the waitress left to fill his order, Suzanne asked, "Where are you from?"

"A demon realm," he answered much too seriously. Then he broke into a teasing smile. "But I picked up the accent in Georgia. What about you?"

"California girl. Born and bred." She gave her dress a little tug, making it more presentable. "And I'm a fashion designer. What do you do for a living?"

"I'm a singer, songwriter, and guitar man."

A musician. She should have guessed. "Where did you meet your friends?"

"We connected on the streets when we were teenagers. Tough-ass runaways and all that."

He glanced away as if he were impatient for his beer. But she could tell that it was an excuse to avoid a discussion about his youth. Kids didn't normally run away unless something was seriously wrong at home.

She let him off the hook. "It's all right. We can talk about something else."

He shifted his gaze back to her, and she thought about her own youth. She'd come from a dysfunctional family and preferred not to dwell on it, either.

"We could talk about how I'm going to turn you into a really bad girl," he said.

She laughed. "You're certainly off to a good start."

"You're easy prey."

His remark should have bothered her, but she let it go. He was pretending to be a demon, after all.

The waitress arrived with his beer, and he thanked her and patted her rear. The girl wiggled her ass in happy response and took off to do her job.

Okay, now Suzanne bristled. "I hate it when guys flirt with other women in front of me."

He made a perplexed expression, and she realized he'd never been in anything that remotely resembled a relationship.

"Never mind," she said.

Like the sexy scoundrel he was, he poured on the southern charm. "I'm sorry, Susie Q. I'll do better next time."

She shook her head. "You don't have a clue how to behave yourself."

"No, I suppose I don't." He pulled on his beer. "And that's why girls like you shouldn't play with boys like me."

"I'm holding my own." She stated the obvious. "I let you put your hand up my dress, didn't I?"

"Yes, ma'am, you did." He leaned toward her, his spicy scent filling her senses. "And for your reward, I'm going to take you out to dinner next week. To a really fancy place, and while we're waiting for our sweet-and-creamy dessert to arrive, I'm going to unzip my pants and you're going to stroke my cock."

A moan escaped her lips. Was this a fantasy he was creating or was he actually going to take her on a dirty date? Either way, she played along. "What if you come? Won't that get messy?"

"I'll make you stop before that happens." He kissed her soft and slow, intensifying the already scorching heat between them.

As he toyed lustfully with her tongue, she hoped that he was serious about the dinner date. She wanted to go out with him.

He ended the kiss and sat back in his chair to finish his beer. Following suit, she sipped the drink Damien had ordered. She vaguely recalled him and Auntie Em leaving the table, but she'd been otherwise engaged.

"Do you want to watch other people mess around?" Jake asked. "The voyeur rooms are on the second floor."

"Do the people in those rooms know they're being spied on?"

He nodded. "Everything that goes on at the club is consensual. Some of the screening windows are out in the open, but I prefer the private viewing areas."

"I'm game for whatever you normally do." She shouldn't be, but she was. Jake and his dark eyes were addictive.

They headed upstairs. The second floor bustled with voyeurs gathered in front of glass partitions that showcased public fucking and sucking.

"Where are the private areas?" she asked.

"This way." As they passed a trio of bleached blondes scribbling something on a graffiti-covered wall, he said, "That's a groupie tradition around here. You can write something on it later if you want."

"Like what?" She bumped his shoulder. "'Jake corrupted Suzanne here.'"

He smiled. "That sounds good to me. So, what do you want to watch? Couples, threesomes, or orgy-type action?"

"I don't know." It was all madly exciting. "You pick."

"Individual couples is more intimate."

"Then let's do that."

She waited while he went up and down the hall, searching for a private viewing area that wasn't occupied. When he found one, he motioned for her to join him. They went inside and locked the door. Although the space was relatively small and dimly lit, it contained a floor-to-ceiling window displaying an ostentatious bedroom on the other side. Fascinated, she walked up to the window and touched the glass.

"It's a one-way mirror," Jake told her. "Glass on our side and a mirror on theirs. It creates a sense of realism for the couple who's being watched. We can see them, but they can't see us."

At the moment, the room was empty. "There's no one there."

"It's a little early. They're not scheduled for another fifteen minutes or so."

"How do you know when they'll show up?"

"Bedrooms are reserved ahead of time. I checked the schedule before we came in."

She gazed through the window once again. Bold lighting lent the atmosphere an art nouveau quality, and a four-poster bed draped in crushed velvet added a Gothic touch.

"Will they have the room the entire night?" she asked, wondering about the mystery couple who had yet to enter.

"Not the entire night, but until the club closes. Then it'll be cleaned and refreshed for the next couple who reserves it." He moved in to stand behind her. "Are you anxious to watch?"

"Yes." Much too anxious.

"Me, too." He unzipped the back of her dress.

"What are you doing?"

"Taking this off."

He slid the dress down her body and helped her step out of it. She waited for him to unhook her bra, but he left it in place, along with her panties and platforms heels. Aside from stripping her down to her lingerie and gently looping his arms around her, he didn't make a sexual advance.

Steeped in anticipation, they remained quiet until a delicate woman in a sparkling-winged costume entered the bedroom.

"It's starting," he said.

Suzanne's breath rushed out. She hadn't expected the supernatural to be female, much less a waiflike fairy with white blonde hair, a heart-shaped face, and a flowing kerchief dress. "She's beautiful."

"Do you think her groupie will be a man or another woman?"

"I don't know." She hadn't considered the possibility that the couple might be the same sex, even if the club catered to straight, bi, gay, and lesbian lovers.

The fairy walked right up to the window, and Suzanne flinched.

"It's okay." Jake eased her back against him. "She can't see us, remember? She's just looking at herself in the mirror."

"But she knows that someone is probably here."

"That's part of the thrill. Knowing but not knowing."

The fairy reached up and removed a silver comb from her hair, then fluffed her pale locks. Watching her prepare herself for her lover was exhilarating. When she wet her sugar pink lips, Suzanne ran her tongue across her own lips.

Then the groupie walked in.

It was a man, and he was as tall and tan as the woman was petite and fair. His attire was simple by comparison: slightly frayed jeans and a tight black shirt that accentuated his broad frame.

"Damn," Jake said.

Yes, damn. She couldn't wait to see what was going to happen next.

Finally the fairy acknowledged the groupie, and he moved forward. They gazed at each other for what seemed like an emotional moment. She said something to him, but their words weren't audible through the glass.

Suzanne could hear Jake breathing behind her. She could feel his aroused energy, too.

The fairy removed her wings, then shed her filmy dress. She was naked underneath, and not only did her skin shimmer with body glitter, the areolas around her tiny breasts were decorated with faceted gems. When she presented her backside to the glass, Suzanne noticed that she had an extra set of wings tattooed across her shoulder blades and down her spine, with the tips ending at her tailbone.

"Are you enjoying this?" Jake asked.

"Yes." She'd never imagined a more sensual scene.

The big man lifted his tiny lover up, and she put her arms around his neck and folded her legs around his waist. They nuzzled and kissed.

"I'm glad we're doing this," Jake said.

Mesmerized, she responded, "So am I."

The other couple kissed and kissed, then he set her back on her feet and cupped her jeweled breasts. That prompted Jake to reach into Suzanne's bra and tease her nipples.

Heaven on earth. How could someone portraying something as dark as a demon have such a light touch?

He shifted his caressing hands to her stomach, and her entire body tingled. By now, the groupie had dropped to his knees to lick the fairy's navel.

The man moved lowered, and Jake whispered, "There he goes."

Yes, there he went, right to his lover's cunt. He opened her up and ran his tongue up and down her labia. She tugged him closer, and he ate her in earnest, making hard, hungry love to her with his mouth.

Jake slipped his hand into Suzanne's panties and fingered her clit, making her skin turn slick and hot.

The activity behind the glass got wilder. The fairy pushed at the groupie's shoulders, indicating for him to lie on the floor. Then, while he was on the ground, she straddled his face and rocked her shimmering body back and forth, arching and bucking as if he were a pony.

Jake hissed. "She's a wild little thing."

Wild and greedy. Suzanne's knees actually went weak. Behind her, Jake was hard and pressed against her butt. Unable to help herself, she reached back to undo his pants.

"That feels good, Susie Q." He nudged her hand away. "But you can't unzip me until our date."

"So, you're really going to take me out?"

"Of course I am. You're my new plaything." He directed her attention back to the bedroom scene. "And someday you're going to sit on my face like that."

Someday? Someday when? She watched the fairy lift herself up just enough to look down at her lover while she juiced up his mouth. Was she moaning? Was she making sweet, naughty noises?

As Jake rubbed Suzanne even harder, forcing her into a heart-thundering orgasm, the fairy came, too, shaking and shuddering in carnal spasms.

Soon the other man stood up, and Jake removed his hand from Suzanne's cream-soaked panties.

In the aftermath, she considered how easily she kept giving herself to him. What'd he'd said was true: she was his new plaything. But everything about their impending relationship was just a dirty game.

A sexual derailing, she thought, as he reached for her again, and they waited for the groupie to climb out of his clothes and fuck the fairy.

Five

Was this as kinky as it seemed? Jane asked herself.

Of course it was, her logical mind answered, but it was also hands-on research. Very hands on, she surmised, as Marcus continued to stand behind her with his arms looped around her waist.

Leaning back against him, she watched the slave fight her bonds as she fought her orgasm. Between the suction cups attached to her nipples and the vibrator buzzing between her legs, the poor girl didn't have a chance.

Jane had a vibrator at home. A different model, but a feel-good device just the same. Maybe she would use it later tonight. Maybe she would press it against her clit and—

"You're enjoying this," Marcus said.

Yes, she was, and far too much. Struggling with the feeling, she attempted to take a cleansing breath, but all she could smell was sex-laced air.

"I want you to think about your limits, Jane."

How clever he was, starting a conversation like this while she watched another woman being dominated. She tried to stay strong and ignore the heat he incited, but instead of pulling away, she leaned back even farther against him.

Then she asked, "What sorts of things do you want to do to me?"

"Besides clamping your nipples and making you call me sir before I push my cock into your mouth?"

Oh, Lord. "Yes, besides that."

He kissed her bare shoulder, much too tenderly. "I'm into blindfolds. Something soft and silky would look pretty on you."

Intrigued, she closed her eyes. A blindfold actually sounded romantic. "What else?"

"Gags and muzzles."

She opened her eyes. That didn't sound the least bit romantic, but she was still intrigued. "To keep me quiet while you do bad things to me?"

"Good things," he corrected. "I don't inflict bad pain. Only good."

"There's a difference?"

"Good pain is within a sub's limits."

Like having her nipples clamped? Or being gagged? Or letting him thrust his cock into her mouth? Were those rough acts within her limits?

He spoke quietly in her ear. "It was kismet that we met."

She didn't want to think about him in terms of fate. "It was a chance encounter."

"I don't believe in chance. Everything happens for a reason."

"And you think the reason we met is because I'm supposed to become your new sub?"

Rather than respond, he kissed her shoulder again, only this time he tightened his hold. The dual sensation, the pressure of being restricted in his arms while he did something soft with his mouth was almost more than she could bear.

Cripes, but she wanted to see the slave come. By now, the other woman was begging for mercy, prompting her devious master to turn the vibrator to a higher speed.

Marcus released his hold on Jane, making her want to beg him to restrict her again. Beg and beg, just like the moaning, thrashing slave chained to the wall.

While she watched, the other woman threw her head back. Then, drenched in pleasure too intense to deny, the captive bit down on her bottom lip, drawing a bit of blood.

Jane nearly bit her lip, too. The sweet little slave was coming like a geyser, the orgasm spilling over her bondage-bound body in waves.

Marcus said, "Just think of how easily that could be you."

Jane's heart went haywire. "Is he going to punish her now?"

"I would if I were him."

Clock-ticking silence passed, intensifying the anticipation.

Then, finally, the warlock walked away from his slave to retrieve a black satchel that had been tucked away in a corner of the cell. Reaching inside, he removed a short, small whip with a slew of leather tassels.

Jane sucked in her breath, and Marcus said, "That's a gentle flogger. See how thick the tress bundle is? That creates less of a sting."

"Do you use that type?"

"Why? Do you want me to give you a gentle flogging? Or would you rather I bend you over my knee and use something with more bite?"

"Like what?" she dared to ask.

"A riding crop would do nicely."

She pictured him dressed in breeches and knee-high boots, using his instrument of choice and leaving telltale marks on her ass. And because the image excited her, she warned herself to get a grip. She was in no frame of mind to think about being punished, not while the warlock was—

Snap!

He slapped the flogger against the top of his slave's mound, and Jane gasped.

Snap! Snap!

Two more lashes. Dizzy with want, Jane feared she might pitch herself against the cell. And do what? Come all over the bars?

To combat the feeling, she spun around and faced Marcus. "That's a gentle flogging?"

"It creates more noise than pain. But you like the noise. You like all of it."

"I don't like liking it."

"Eventually you will."

After another thundering snap, she nearly lost what was left of her bondage-wracked mind. All she could think about was Marcus branding her with a riding crop.

Overwhelmed, she said, "I think I should find my friends and go home."

"Right now?"

"Yes." Right now, before she offered herself to him.

"Okay. But when you're ready to experiment, I want you to call me." He removed a business card from his pocket and slipped it into her hand.

Avoiding his gaze, she glanced down at it. His full name was Marcus Monroe. AKA: Master Monroe.

He escorted her out of the community playroom, and as they approached the hallway with the medieval torture devices on the wall, she could feel him watching her with those hypnotic eyes.

She stared straight ahead.

They continued through the mazelike hallways, and when they reached the reception area where the clit girl and the were-wolf guy had been, Jane remained silent.

After exiting the dungeon, they went upstairs because Marcus claimed that he had a pretty good idea of where her friends might be.

They located Suzanne on the second floor with Jake, where she was writing on a graffiti-littered wall. As for Emily, they found her and Damien on the third floor surrounded by erotic art.

"We'll walk you to the parking lot." Marcus spoke on behalf of the men.

Jane spoke for the women. "We'll be fine by ourselves."

Out of the corner of her eye, she saw Suzanne and Jake French kissing like fiends. He had his hands firmly planted on her butt, too. There was nothing subtle about their good-bye.

Jane glanced at Emily. She and Damien weren't touching, but lust-lorn energy buzzed between them.

"Sizing everyone up?" Marcus asked.

She turned her attention back to him. "If it wasn't for my article, we wouldn't have come here. I feel responsible."

"For what? Making hot things happen?" He skimmed her cheek. "It was meant to be. For all of you."

Jane didn't respond, but she feared that after tonight none of them would ever be the same.

Emily couldn't stop obsessing about Damien. But she suspected that Suzanne and Jane weren't faring much better. After they left the club, they'd returned to Jane's apartment and gathered in the living room, where they sipped steaming cups of white peach tea and stared at each other.

Finally Emily said, "What are we getting ourselves into?"

Suzanne responded, "I don't know, but I can't wait to see Jake next week. There's just something about him that makes me want to do really dirty things." She winced a little. "But I guess you already saw the kind of stuff he inspires me to do."

Emily decided not to reprimand her for the table incident. She had carnal woes of her own. "Damien is attracted to what he considers my innocence, and that makes me feel like a sacrificial lamb. But I still want to be with him."

"You think you have problems?" Jane shifted uncomfortably in her chair. "I got turned on watching a master flog a slave, and I got even more excited thinking about Marcus cracking a riding crop across my oh-so-tender ass."

Suzanne had the gall to giggle. But so did Emily. It was all too insane not to laugh. Even Jane joined in.

Then they went sober.

Jane said, "Marcus is an erotic hypnotist, and he thinks that I have repressed fantasies about becoming sexually submissive."

"Do you?" Suzanne asked.

"I don't know, but it sure feels like it."

Emily interjected, "He could've hypnotized you into believing that's what you want."

"I thought about that. In fact, I worried about it for most of the evening. But I still don't trust myself to stay away from him."

Which was a dilemma each of them faced, Emily thought. No matter how hard she tried to reject Damien in her mind, images of being his lover slid through her body like a silk-weaving snake. Before they'd parted ways, he'd convinced her to program his number into her cell phone. "It's as if they put a spell on us."

Suzanne lifted her tea from the coffee table. "Jake told me that they met on the streets when they were teenagers. That they were 'tough-ass' runaways. But I didn't press him for more information. I could tell he didn't want to talk about his youth."

Jane remarked, "I'm not surprised that they came from the streets. It's probably where they learned to be so aggressive." She went on to say, "Do you know what Marcus told me? That some of the club goers believe that there are actually real supernaturals who frequent Aeonian, and according to gossip, one of our guys is the genuine article and the other two are protecting his secret."

A sudden chill raced through Emily's blood.

Jane continued, "After he told me about the rumors, he teased me about how he had a demonic side in bed."

Emily couldn't help the next words that spilled from her mouth. "What if it's true?"

"That he has a demonic side in bed? I don't doubt that."

"That isn't what I meant." Wishing she'd never gone to the club, that she'd never laid eyes on that unholy place, she fought another chill. "What if one of them really is a demon?"

Jane all but gaped at her. "Oh, my goodness. Do you realize how ridiculous that sounds?"

"Yes, but . . ."

"But nothing. They're men. Flesh and blood, like everyone else at Aeonian."

Now that Emily thought about it, Damien had made a similar claim, telling her that he and his friends were men, not monsters. But what would stop a demon from lying?

"It could be Damien," she said, determined to make her ridiculous point. "He has the same name as the *Omen* kid, he paints demonic things, and when he smiles, he looks like a fallen angel." She omitted the left-handed part because she knew that would sound even dumber.

Suzanne burst into a silly smile. "Really, Auntie Em. Why should you get to have all the fun? If any of them is a demon, it's Jake. When I asked him where he was from, he joked around and said that he hailed from a demon realm. But what if he actually meant it?" She fluttered the hem of her dress and pretended to flash her panties. "And he was the quickest to cast his net. Just think of how he's making me misbehave."

"Are you kidding?" Jane got in on the humor. "My guy is a better candidate. He's the one who mentioned the real demon thing to begin with, and he's an erotic hypnotist who binds, blindfolds, and gags his lovers." She lifted her rear and playfully smacked the side of it. "I'm already turning into his ass-whipped slave."

SHERI WHITEFEATHER

"Okay, fine." Emily laughed. How could she not? "But I still think we should be careful."

Just in case.

For the past week, Suzanne had worked like a maniac at her job, keeping herself busy and waiting for her date with Jake.

And now the time had come.

She paced her apartment and glanced at her watch. Was she really going to unzip his pants while waiting for their dessert to be served? She normally didn't even eat dessert. Yeah, well, she didn't normally stroke her date's cock under the table, either.

Nonetheless, she'd gotten ready for an upscale evening. She'd swept her pale blonde hair away from her face, applied her makeup with elegant precision, and chosen to wear a sparkling little cocktail dress. She'd debated on whether or not to don panties, but in the end, she'd slipped on a sexy thong.

Would Jake be wearing underwear? Or would he go commando to make their naughty game easier?

Anxious for him to arrive, she resisted the urge to peer out the window.

Suddenly the doorbell chimed, sending her heart lunging for her throat. Taking a moment to breathe, she smoothed her dress and headed toward the summons.

She opened the door and there stood Jake, nicely attired. He smiled, and she invited him inside. Once they were in her living room and she could see him in a brighter light, she noticed that he was wearing the black contact lenses.

"Are we going to the club after dinner?" she asked.

"No."

She gestured to his eyes. "Then why are you still in supernatural mode?"

"I always wear these, and so do Marcus and Damien. It started off as a gimmick, even before we joined the club. We did it to add a bit a mystery to our professional images: me with my music, Marcus with his hypnotism, and Damien with his art. And now that we've been wearing them for so long, it's become part of who we are."

She couldn't fault them for having a gimmick. She often wondered what she could do to make herself more noticeable in the fashion world.

"So, what's your music like, Jake?"

"Sometimes I write sexually charged lyrics, and sometimes I write songs that pit good against evil."

That made sense, considering his darkly erotic lifestyle. "I'd love to see you perform sometime."

"I do studio work. I sing backup and play guitar on other artist's recordings."

"Then what about the songs you write?"

"They're just for me. My poetry, I guess. I don't have the

desire to record them. Speaking of desire . . ." He turned primal, running his gaze over the length of her. "You look hot."

She checked out his tall, broad frame. "So do you."

After a moment of admiring each other, he asked, "Are you ready to go?"

She nodded, and they left her apartment and walked through the courtyard and out to the street where he was parked. His vehicle was a sleek black sedan with wire wheels. He'd obviously put some money into it.

As they merged into traffic, he played music that he'd downloaded on his iPod, and the first song that came on was the Charlie Daniels Band grinding out "The Devil Went Down to Georgia."

Suzanne shot Jake a sideways glance. The song was about the devil challenging a young fiddle player in Georgia to a fiddle-playing contest in order to procure his soul. The plot also involved a band of demon musicians accompanying the devil.

"Interesting song choice," she said. Particularly since Jake had told her that he'd picked up his accent in Georgia.

He stopped at a red light. "The devil gets defeated in it."

"I know." She studied his profile. "What happens in the songs you write for yourself? Does good win over evil?"

He reached over to touch her hand. "Would it make a difference?"

"No." At the moment all she cared about was being near him. "But it probably would to Emily. She got a little worried that the rumors about you and Marcus and Damien might be true."

"No one is a demon. That's just crazy club talk."

"You don't have to convince me. I think it's impossible."

After their conversation ended, he turned up the music. And when the light changed, he punched the gas pedal, accelerating into the night.

Six

I wonder how Suzanne is doing on her date," Emily said.

"Better than we are, I'm sure." Jane gazed at the hamburger and fries in front of her. With nothing to do on a Friday night, she and Auntie Em had ended up at an overcrowded diner.

Emily sucked on her milk shake. "Maybe we should go to a movie after this."

"What do you want to see?"

Another hard suck. "I don't know."

"Me, neither. And will you quit with the milk shake. You look like you're trying to give your straw a blow job."

"It's not my fault." The brunette made a face. "It's too thick." She gave up and tried to stir it with a too-short spoon. "This is annoying."

"So is this." Jane pounded on the side of the ketchup bottle, but nothing came out. "Hasn't this dive ever heard of those new-fangled contraptions called squeeze jars?"

"What's wrong with us?" Emily asked, then said, "Never mind. Dumb question. Those men are what's wrong."

Yes, Jane thought. Hot men. Powerful men. Wild, wild men. "I'm still having fantasies about wanting Marcus to whip me, and I'm terrified of letting something like that happen. Yet I'm desperate to call him." She pounded on the bottle again. "How mixed up am I?"

"Do you know what I did this morning? I Googled the name 'Damien.'"

"Just to be sure it doesn't mean child of the devil?" A bloody-looking glob of ketchup finally came out. "So what does it mean?"

"It has Greek origins and it means 'to tame.'" Emily crinkled her forehead. "That would have made me feel better if Damien hadn't asked me if I thought the maiden in one of his paintings should tame the demon who was stalking her." She leaned forward. "I don't want him to be a demon, and I don't want to be the innocent maiden he's stalking."

"I thought we already established that none of them is a real supernatural."

"I'm still skeptical."

Rather than rehash the same argument, Jane said, "I'd rather be with a demon who longs to be tamed than one who hypnotizes women into becoming his slaves."

Emily frowned. "Does Marcus have a gentle side? Or did he seem dangerous the entire time you were in the dungeon with him?"

"He was both."

"Do you think you're going to call him?"

"Probably."

"Once you do, it'll be too late to turn back."

"I know." But she couldn't think of another way to curb her craving for him. She'd gone to bed each night this week with him on her mind, and she woke up the same way.

Because there didn't seem to be much else to say, Jane glanced out the window and gazed at the shrubbery alongside the building.

Then Emily popped off with an in-depth question. "What do you think would happen if one of us fell in love with one of them?"

Heaven have mercy. "Don't even go there."

"I was just wondering."

"You shouldn't be thinking about things like that." Particularly when Jane was on the verge of calling Marcus. "We've been saddled with enough temptation."

Way more than they could handle.

The dimly lit décor sparkled with lush woods and beveled mirrors. Centerpieces consisted of etched-glass jars, brimming with floating candles.

Suzanne and Jake sat side by side at a corner table, which he'd apparently requested because it was a lovely little linen-draped booth that provided a measure of privacy. But Suzanne was still anxious. She couldn't stop thinking about dessert even though they were only on the salad.

She glanced around at the other patrons. Would any of them notice that something "funny" was going on later? That the couple in the corner was getting a tad too amorous?

"Have you ever done this here before?" she asked.

"Done what? Have dinner?"

"Don't tease me. You know what I mean."

"This is the first time I've been here. But I checked it out ahead of time. It seemed like a really nice place."

It was, extremely nice. But it was also quiet and conservative. "We're too noticeable, Jake."

"What do you mean?"

"You with your Gothic vibe and me with my tight little cocktail dress. We don't blend in."

"It'll be fine. This is L.A. We're not the only noticeable people out there."

Yes, but how many of them messed around in classy restaurants? While she stumbled through her salad, he ate his without a hitch.

She said, "At least we're going to look stylish in our mug shots."

He laughed. "You worry too much."

"What we're planning to do is called lewd and lascivious conduct."

"I know what it's called." He sipped his lemon-garnished

water. "But isn't that term kind of redundant? Doesn't lewd and lascivious mean the same thing? They're both synonymous with wicked, lustful, unchaste . . ."

Suzanne dropped the conversation, and by time their entrees arrived, she did her best to behave as if she were on a proper date. She took ladylike bites of mushroom risotto and sipped courage-building chardonnay. Jake wasn't drinking. Clearly, he didn't need spirits to help him relax.

As candlelight flickered in his eyes and created a reflective spark, she asked, "Who started the rumor about you and Marcus and Damien?"

"I don't know. But rumors are common at Aeonian. We're not the only members accused of being real."

"Yes, but in your case, it's interesting how it's only supposed to be one of you and not all three."

"That's because three is a symbolic number, and some people think that three demons would never appear together in public. According to the rumor, we would be too obvious in threes, and it would be impossible for us to hide who and what we are."

"What's so powerful about the number three?"

"The Holy Trinity, for one. For another, Jesus is said to have died at three p.m. and ascended into heaven on the third day." Jake gave a slight pause. "Demonic rituals are often conducted at three a.m. because it's the opposite of three p.m., and some people think that the veil between this world and the dark realm can be penetrated at that hour."

"I suspect that the three of you wearing your contact lenses outside the club probably fuels the rumors, too."

"You're right, that's part of it. But why spoil the mystery after all these years?"

Caught up in it, she asked, "What color are your eyes without them?"

"What color do you think they are?"

She studied his wildly handsome features. Blue would complement his natural blonde hair, but so would a light shade of brown, or green, or maybe a combination like hazel. "I don't know."

He didn't say anything, and she became immersed in the quiet, wondering how it would feel to curl up beside him or put her head in the crook of his shoulder and fall asleep in his arms.

"What are you thinking about, Suzanne?"

She snapped out of the gentle musing. The last thing she needed was to have romantic fantasies about a man who'd called her his plaything.

"I'm thinking about dessert," she said.

"Then finish your risotto so we can order it."

She glanced at his plate. His pasta was almost gone. She ate a few more bites of her food. "What kind of dessert do you think we should get?"

"Chocolate soufflé. It's served with crème fraîche ice cream and takes about fifteen minutes to make."

"How do you know how long it takes?"

"I already checked this place out beforehand, remember?"

"Yes, of course." He wouldn't have left the most significant part of their meal to chance.

"Fifteen minutes is plenty of time for us to play around. More than enough for you to make me hard."

She suspected that he was already half hard just thinking about it. Obeying his command, she finished her entree, and he smiled.

Soon their plates were cleared, and they ordered the chocolate soufflé. After the waiter departed, she looked around at the other patrons, as she'd done earlier.

"They don't matter," Jake told her.

"Yes, they do." It was the other people's proximity that made the game so powerful.

He scooted closer to her. "How we feel is all that matters."

Wild? Decadent? Aroused? Beneath the table, she put her hand on his thigh and heard him suck in his breath. She inched closer to his fly.

"Keep going," he whispered.

She fumbled with the button, and he reached down to help her, like a teenage boy encouraging a hesitant girl.

Together they unzipped his trousers, and he took his hand away, leaving the rest up to her. She worked her way down, getting past the hem of his shirt. He wasn't wearing underwear and his pubic region was free of hair. She assumed that he kept it smooth for moments like this, making it easier for a woman to glide her hand along his skin. Within an instant, Suzanne connected with his cock.

As she'd suspected, he was half hard. He jerked his hips, and she traced the tip with her thumb. Nothing had ever seemed so wrong yet so dangerously right.

Voices hummed in the background. She heard the soft clink of glassware, too. At another table, someone was making an elegant toast. In the midst of it all, Suzanne curled her fingers around Jake's penis and stroked him ever so lightly.

"Good girl," he said, getting harder.

Furthering her quest, she increased the motion, and he took the opportunity to kiss her on the mouth. But he made it quick, leaving them both hungry for more.

Suddenly the waiter approached a nearby table, and her heart skipped a thousand beats. "What should I do?"

"Exactly what you're doing. It feels good."

She continued touching him, and as the waiter tended to other patrons, Jake pushed deeper into her hand, heightening the thrill.

"Are you going to fuck me tonight?" she asked.

"No, but I'm going to go home and jerk off while I'm thinking about you."

Her pussy clenched. She thoroughly liked that idea. "For real?"

"Hell, yes." He opened his legs a bit wider, giving her even more room under the table.

She noticed the maître d' across the room. She saw a busboy refilling water glasses, too. Lord, this was dirty. And so damned crazy.

Jake said, "The minute I get home I'm going to shove my pants down and have at it. And I'm going to pretend that you're there, getting ready to kneel over my face."

She gripped him tighter. She longed to do exactly what he described.

He continued his erotic tale. "In my fantasy, you'll peel off your panties and hike up your dress. Then you'll straddle me and move closer, showing me your swollen little clit."

With her hand wrapped firmly around his cock, and her cunt getting creamy, she looked into his fathomless eyes.

Heaven help her, but she liked playing around in public, especially while he spun wicked stories. She wanted to do this again and again, in all sorts of taboo locations. She gave his penis a hard tug, and he made a rough sound.

"You need to stop now, Suzanne."

She didn't want to let go. "Are you sure?"

His body nearly shuddered. "Positive."

She released him, and they blinked at each other. Then he grabbed his water and took a long swig. While he got control of his senses and zipped his fly, she felt as sinful as the dessert that was still on its way.

The thick, rich soufflé that arrived just minutes later.

Seven

Jane called Marcus on Saturday afternoon. And now, on Saturday evening, she rode in the backseat of a taxi, en route to the club. Initially, she intended to take her own car. But Marcus claimed that some subs got "spacey" after a first-time BDSM experience, so she might not be in the frame of mind to drive herself home. She didn't see herself as the spacey type, but who the hell knew? None of this was within her normal behavior, except, as usual, she was running late.

Beyond nervous, she fidgeted with her hands, locking her fingers, then unlocking them. Marcus would be waiting for her at the street-level entrance to the club. She couldn't meet him inside because she didn't have a guest pass for tonight. She'd acquired the previous passes from a friend of a friend. This time, Marcus would be providing one.

A short while later, as the cabbie headed toward Aeonian, she spotted Marcus's tall, regal frame.

After the driver pulled over to the curb, she paid the fare and got out. Marcus approached her, and she noticed that he was dressed in a similar manner as before, with an impeccable white shirt and long-tailed jacket. She tried not to marvel at how mysterious he looked under the glow of scattered streetlights. A portion of his sleek black hair fell in shadow, as did his piercing eyes.

"Hello, Lady Jane."

Could he be any more fascinating? "That's not my nickname."

"I think it suits you. You're especially lovely tonight."

"Thank you." Her groupie gear consisted of a lacy top, no bra, a skintight skirt, and stiletto heels. She valued the extra height around him.

"I didn't get you a guest pass," he said. "I bought you a membership instead."

"You shouldn't have done that."

"I wanted to. Besides, you're going to need regular access to the club for us to form a relationship."

She glanced at the iron fence that secured the front of the building. This entrance seemed much more foreboding than the way in through the parking lot. "How long is the membership good for?"

"Six months."

Was he expecting her to be his sub for all that time? "That sounds like a commitment on my part."

"If you're concerned about it seeming too exclusive, you can help me form a harem."

"You mean pick other women out for you?"

"A group of subs often serve one dominant. Or they can serve multiple dominants. But I don't like to share with other doms."

"What if I don't want to share with other subs?"

He reached out to touch a strand of her hair. She'd worn it long and loose, but she'd added a bit of flair with a jeweled comb.

"If me having a harem isn't acceptable to you, then we'll have to remain exclusive for a while, won't we?"

Did he just trick her into a commitment? Or was she tripping herself up with refusing to share?

He ran a finger across the comb. "Did you wear this pretty bauble for me?"

"Yes," she said stupidly. She'd worn everything for him.

He reached into his coat pocket and removed a slim leather collar, decorated with metal ornaments and a D-ring in the center. "This will help you adjust to the role of being submissive." He extended the item toward her and asked, "May I?"

His trance-inducing tone was dangerous in itself, but combined with his ebony stare, it was downright lethal.

Objecting didn't seem like an option. She nodded her approval, and he attached the collar around her neck. The last time she was here, she'd seen other subs sporting them.

"It looks good on you," he said.

"It feels okay." Similar to a choker necklace or a taut strand of pearls.

"This goes with it." He produced a leather leash from the same pocket. "If you don't mind, of course."

Jane's pulse spiked.

"It's common in the dungeon," he told her.

"I know." She was aware that some of the collared subs she'd seen had been leashed. "But are you sure that being led around the club is going to help me adjust?"

"It's symbolic of being owned. And I promise I won't tug on the leash. Too hard," he added with a wry smile.

"I must be going insane."

"Does that mean I have your permission?"

"Yes."

"I booked us an individual playroom. Unless you would prefer to use the community playroom."

With other masters and groupies watching? She might be losing her mind, but she wasn't crazy enough to put herself on display. "I'd rather be in a private setting."

"That's what I figured. I think it's best if we discuss how the scene will play out before we go inside."

"You mean the things you're going to do to me?"

He nodded. "I brought some of my favorite toys with me and put them in a cabinet in the room I reserved. The room is stocked with whips, too. But it's too soon to use any of them."

After he'd taunted her with the idea? After he'd made her crave it? "But I've been fantasizing about the riding crop we talked about."

"Fantasy isn't the same as reality. If I used a crop on you tonight, you'd panic."

"What if I panic about things you think I'm ready for?"

"Then you can let me know how you feel with a safe word. I'll provide you with two safe words—one that stops the scene entirely and another that communicates a willingness to continue, but at a reduced level of intensity."

"Why can't I just say 'stop the scene' or 'don't do that'?"

"Because when you're in the moment, you might plead with me to stop or slow down without actually meaning it. Safe words avoid confusion."

"What if I don't want to call you 'sir'?"

"That's nonnegotiable." He moved forward and jiggled her leash. "Shall we go?"

She took a step toward him, then stalled. Was she actually getting involved with a man portraying a demon, a man who probably knew every dirty BDSM trick in the book?

He raised his brows at her. "Is there a problem?"

Yes, she thought. But she said, "No," and followed him to the iron gate.

He used his keycard to open it, and after he presented her brand-new membership card to the girl manning the lobby desk, he took Jane to the dungeon.

When they arrived at the private playroom he'd reserved, he unlocked the door and they went inside.

The room boasted shiny wood floors and rugged bondage equipment. One of the walls was completely mirrored, magnifying the view. Another wall contained a collection of artfully displayed whips and floggers. She caught sight of a slim black riding crop among them, but she did her best to ignore it.

Marcus led her to a set of chains and manacles suspended from the ceiling. She glanced up and noticed that the chains were on a pulley system. He removed her leash and tucked it into his pocket. She waited to see what he would do next, but he didn't do anything except step back and look at her. His mystic-eyed perusal made the pulse between her legs pound. She could see herself in the mirror, along with an imposing reflection of the back of his body.

He said, "The safe words are 'red' and 'yellow.' Red to stop the scene and yellow to proceed with caution. If you're wearing a gag or muzzle and are unable to speak, all you have to do is snap your fingers to get my attention and make me stop."

"Are you planning to use a gag or muzzle tonight?"

"I will if you let me."

Would she? At the moment, she wasn't sure.

He changed the subject. "Are you wearing panties?"

"Yes."

"Take them off and give them to me."

She reached under her skirt, peeled them down, and handed them over.

He slipped them into his pocket with the leash. "Now take off your blouse."

Once again, she did his bidding, then stood before him without her top, her small breasts bared for his entertainment. Already her nipples were hard.

He tossed her blouse onto a piece of nearby equipment and told her to ditch her skirt. "But keep your shoes on," he added.

Jane obeyed his command, and after he discarded her skirt, he gave her another order.

"Lift your arms."

She raised them up, and he adjusted the chains from the ceiling to fit her, then locked her wrists to the fleece-lined manacles.

"Comfy?" he asked.

As comfortable as a naked woman chained to a ceiling could be. "Yes."

"Yes, *sir*," Marcus provided.

"Yes, sir," she repeated, only in a much softer way.

Obviously satisfied with her submissive tone, he walked over to the cabinet he'd stocked with his favorite toys. He returned with a device similar to what the warlock master had used on his slave.

"This is called a spreader bar," he said. "I'm going to attach the cuffs to your ankles and adjust the bar so it keeps your legs in a wide-open stance."

He knelt down, and she cooperated with the position he desired. The cuffs on the bar were gently padded, much like the manacles on her wrists.

Intrigued, she gazed at her reflection. Never in a million years could she have imagined herself this way. But there she was, bound for a man she barely knew.

"Do you like what you see?" Marcus asked.

"Yes." Her nipples remained hard, and her pubic region was a modest triangle. Her wide stance, secured with the spreader bar, enhanced the wickedness of her heels.

"I like what I see, too." He thumbed her breasts. "Do you think I should clamp you?"

She said, "No, sir."

"I agree. At least not this first time. But I do think you should get used to the idea."

To prove his point, he retrieved a silver chain from the cabinet. The chain had a hook in the center and tweezer-style clamps at each end. He fastened the hook to the D-ring on her collar, but he didn't use the clamps on her nipples. He left them dangling between her breasts.

She sighed her relief.

He produced a leather gag with a small phallic-shaped object attached. "The cock is made of rubber and is designed to fit comfortably in a sub's mouth. What do you think? Shall we try it?"

"I don't know."

He held the penis in front of her. "It's only an inch long and three inches in circumference. Surely you can handle that."

No doubt she could. But she still hesitated, uncertain about being silenced.

"I promise to do something special to you if you agree to wear it. Something you'll really like."

Curious to let him continue, she took the deepest breath possible, like a swimmer preparing for a dive. "Go ahead and do it."

He pushed the phallus into her mouth, filling her with the taste of rubber. As he fastened the leather strap, she dared a glance at herself, startled by how vulnerable she looked.

Once the gag was in place, he headed toward the whips. Jane watched his every move. Had he lied? Was he going to use the riding crop on her?

Sure enough, he removed it from the wall. Flicking his wrist, he tested the implement, making it snap in the air. The motion caused Jane to flinch. The panic he'd mentioned earlier was setting in. She didn't want to be whipped.

Should she snap her fingers and end the madness? Or should she wait and see what his next move was?

Crazy as it was, she waited.

He turned to look at her. "Do you ride? I do. But I prefer English over Western. When you mount a horse in English, you hold the crop in your left hand." He demonstrated. "But as you ride, you switch the crop back and forth to your 'inside' hand. That's the hand on the side of the horse that's away from the rail."

She didn't ride and she didn't know how to use a crop. But she wasn't in a position to discuss it with him.

While her heart pounded at an immeasurable speed, he

walked in a circle around her. She watched him in the mirror. He lingered behind her, and she tensed.

"You're afraid I'm going to hit you," he said. "But I told you that I wasn't." Still clutching the whip, he moved to stand in front of her. "You need to learn to trust me ."

Clever dom that he was, he slid the crop along her inner thigh, caressing her with it. As Jane's cunt clenched, she sucked on the rubber cock in her mouth, using it like a pacifier.

Marcus smiled. "Now you're getting turned on."

It annoyed her that he was narrating her feelings. But she couldn't deny the arousal gathering in her loins.

He leaned forward and licked one of her nipples, and the wetness of his tongue created a wondrous shiver. But it also made her aware of the chain attached to her collar and the clamps he'd claimed he wouldn't use.

He licked her other nipple. "Trust me. I won't hurt you."

She was trying to take him at his word, but between the whip and the clamps, he could inflict some serious pain. How could she be sure that he would end the scene if she wanted him to? Being bound and gagged put her in a precarious situation.

He reached around and ran the crop along her butt cheeks and down the back of her thighs, teasing her with the leather again, ever so softly.

"Ah, yes, Lady Jane is enjoying this."

She was. Cripes, how she was. But the fear of being clamped or whipped hadn't gone away.

Keeping the crop handy, he placed it on the ground, right below the spreader bar. Then he got down on his knees, opened her pussy and put his mouth against her.

Thank goodness she hadn't tried to end it.

As he tongue-fucked her, she let the sensation sweep her into a state of bliss. He'd promised something special, but she hadn't counted on him giving her head. Mercy, he was doing it with sweet precision. If she hadn't been restrained, she would've tunneled her hands through his hair; she would have made a physical connection with him.

Jane looked down to watch. By now, her clit was peeking out from its hood like a shiny little pearl. He worked his way toward it, and her legs shuddered.

Lost in the feeling, she made breathy sounds beneath the gag. She never wanted him to stop. Nothing had ever felt so delicious.

"Don't come," he said, jarring her back into the role of being his slave. "Not until I give you permission."

She should have known there was a catch; she should have known that orgasm denial was involved. When she tried to pull her pelvis away from him, he planted his hands on her hips and held her excruciatingly still.

Jane didn't know what to do. Looking at him was making it worse, so she gazed at the mirror. But that only heightened her fear. If she came too soon, would he punish her?

She squeezed her eyes shut, trying to stop the pressure from escalating. But it didn't work. Her pussy was so wet, so slick and creamy, all she wanted was to come.

But he hadn't given her permission.

Don't let it happen, she told herself. Mind over matter.

Marcus went for the kill. While he licked her clit, he thrust a finger inside her, too. One. Then two . . .

She opened her eyes. Hot and sticky, her juices flowed, dripping into his mouth and coating his fingers.

She was close. Too damn close.

She waited for his permission. But he didn't give it.

Her body was unraveling at the seams, and he was relentless, pushing her further and further toward the need for redemption.

As she fought her orgasm, the chains swayed and clanked, reminding her that she was his prisoner. Her breathing quickened, and suddenly the gag seemed too tight. In her delirium, she imagined that Marcus was pushing his cock into her mouth.

Forcing her to suck him.

That did it. Jane lost the battle. She moaned and thrashed and tightened her ass, thrusting her cunt closer to his face. With a muffled cry, she came all over him.

In the aftermath, her heart rattled inside her chest. Marcus wiped the back of his hand across his lips and stood up.

They stared at each other, and she felt as if she were floating. Was this the "spacey" feeling he'd told her about? She felt drunk or drugged or a bit of both.

Without saying anything, he released the spreader bar, removed the gag, and unchained her. Dizzy, she gulped air into her lungs and literally fell into his arms.

He held her close. He stroked a hand down her hair, too, petting her like a kitten. "Next time I'm going to make you pay for disobeying me. Next time you won't get away with this."

She put her head on his shoulder. She liked that he was protecting her. But she could tell that he meant what he said. Next time she was going to feel her master's wrath.

Good and hard.

Eight

The patio yielded Emily's herbs. Some bloomed in clay pots and others grew in wire baskets. Mostly she used them for cooking, but sometimes she brewed fragrant teas. Whether it was a warm summer day or a cool winter night, this was her favorite spot in her apartment.

On this lazy afternoon, she rocked in a weathered canopy swing that had belonged to her maternal grandmother, the religious woman who raised her after her parents had died. Grandma was gone now, too. The closest thing Emily had to family was her two best friends.

At the moment, they sat at a glass-topped table across from her, chattering like magpies about their budding affairs.

According to their graphic discussion, Suzanne had put her

hand down Jake's pants during their dinner date, and last night Jane had allowed Marcus to bind and gag her.

"I'm the only decent one here," Emily said, interrupting their sexual ravings.

They turned simultaneously to look at her, and she wanted to bite back the words. Her decency was a façade, because no matter how she sliced it, she was envious of her friends. At least they had the guts to pursue the men who intrigued them.

"I'm sorry," she said. "I didn't mean that the way it sounded. I'm just . . ."

"Conflicted over Damien?" Jane provided.

Emily nodded and glanced around at the plants. Her grandma had taught her about gardening. Grandma had grown all sorts of herbs, but she'd avoided the botanical known as devil's claw, even if it had good medicinal properties.

"You should call him, Auntie Em," Suzanne said. "You should go for it."

"I agree." Jane tucked a strand of auburn hair behind her ear. "I'm nervous about seeing Marcus again, but I'm excited, too. Experimenting with his lifestyle is the most thrilling thing that's ever happened to me."

"Ditto," the fashion designer said. "About doing dirty things with Jake."

Jane spoke again. "Marcus thinks that all of us were destined to meet. At first it bothered me when he said it, especially since I never really believed in fate. But now I'm wondering if he could be right." She leaned forward. "I'm not saying that we're destined to marry them or anything like that. But maybe they're meant to awaken our desires."

"But we hardly know anything about them," Emily said.

Suzanne responded, "Are you still worried about the demon thing? I already told you that Jake explained the theory behind the rumors."

"I know, but that only makes the rumors sound more believable to me. The demonic association with the number three. Three men portraying demons at a sex club. Those same three men wearing dark contacts lenses all the time, even though they know it fuels the rumor. What about the expression that eyes are the windows to the soul? If that's true, then they could be hiding their souls."

Suzanne restated her case. "Think about how compelling black eyes make a hypnotist look. Or how they create a mystical aura around an artist who paints supernatural scenes. Or a studio musician who writes sexy and Gothic songs that he keeps to himself. It's a gimmick that works, and I don't blame them for keeping it going."

Jane added her two cents. "Not only do those dark eyes enhance Marcus's hypnotic appeal, they make him a more powerful-looking master, too. Personally, I think it's kind of hot that he wears them all the time."

"And I still think that one of them could be a demon," Emily said, struggling with her superstitions.

No matter how badly she wanted to be with Damien, she just couldn't bring herself to do it.

In the pitch-black of night, Jane tossed and turned. She glanced at the alarm clock beside her bed and checked the time: 1:59.

Why was she so restless? She wasn't an insomniac. Normally sleep came easier to her. In fact, she could crash out just about anywhere.

She glanced at the clock again. Now it was two on the dot. Thank goodness it wasn't three. In spite of being a non-demon believer, she didn't want to think about that number.

Getting goose-bumpy, Jane turned on the lamp. For someone who scoffed at the occult, she had a case of the heebie-jeebies.

She decided to get out of bed, but once she was up, she wasn't sure what she was going to do. Watch TV? Play on the Internet? Work on the Aeonian article?

Whichever activity she chose, the living room was where her TV and computer were located. As she headed in that direction, her goose bumps got worse.

Just as she flipped on the main light switch, the doorbell rang and she nearly jumped out of her skin.

She crept over to the peephole and looked out. It was Marcus.

Good God. He rang again. If she hadn't already been up, his persistence would have awakened her. She couldn't very well pretend that he wasn't here. She wanted to know what he was trying to pull at this time of night.

She flung open the door.

As usual, he was cloaked in a long-tailed jacket and his shiny black hair was tied back in a ponytail, making his features more prominent.

"Hello, Lady Jane," he said, calm as you please.

She wasn't nearly as calm. "What are you doing here?"

"I had an urge to see you."

And she'd been tossing and turning before he'd appeared. A moment of confusion came over her. Could this be a dream? Just to be sure that she wasn't in the midst of a nightmare and he wasn't a fear-induced illusion, she pushed against his shoulder. He was flesh and bone, all right.

Very real.

She asked, "How did you get my address? I never gave it to you, and I'm not listed."

"Being listed doesn't matter these days. Not with the invention of the Internet." A teasing smile quirked one corner of his lips. "Surely you've heard of it."

"Ha-ha." Her heart hadn't quit pounding.

He looked her up and down. "That's certainly a lovely outfit."

She tugged on her big ratty T-shirt. She felt more vulnerable now than when she'd been naked, bound, and gagged. "I wasn't expecting company."

"Yes, but I'm here now, so invite me in."

"What for?"

"So I can punish you. You know you're anxious for it."

At this hour? Looking the way she did? Her pride stung. "Go home, Marcus. I don't want to be your sub anymore."

"Yes, you do." He reached out and skimmed her cheek. "Come on, Lady Jane. Be good for me."

Did he have to be so persuasive? And did his touch have to make her ache? Like the dumbest, most submissive woman on earth, she allowed him into her house.

He didn't waste a bit of time. In the next take-charge instant he removed his jacket, draping it meticulously over a chair. He also divested himself of his shirt, handling it in the same tidy manner. He left his pants in place, but she could tell that he planned to unzip them when he was good and ready.

He'd been threatening to make her call him "sir" before he pushed his cock into her mouth, but she'd never imagined it happening in her living room in the middle of a sleep-deprived night.

Hell and damnation.

She *was* anxious to be punished, especially in the manner he had in mind.

When he said, "Get on your knees," she dropped right down.

Triumph sounded in his voice. "You really are a good little sub, aren't you."

Eager to obey him and hating herself for it, she lowered her gaze and studied his stylish black boots. They were perfectly polished, but nothing about Marcus was scuffed.

He said, "Tell me why you deserve this. Tell me in a way that makes my cock hard."

She suspected that he was already hard, but she didn't dare sneak a peek at his fly, not until he gave her permission.

She responded, "When you were licking my clit and fucking me with your fingers, I disobeyed you and came when I wasn't supposed to. But it felt so good, I couldn't help it."

"Are you ready for your punishment?"

Her pussy clenched beneath her panties. "Yes."

"Then beg for it."

Her breath hitched. "Please punish me."

"Say it again."

"Please," she implored, wishing she didn't mean it so much. *"Please."*

"Look at me," he said. "But only as far as my zipper."

Eager to see his penis, she followed his command, and while he undid the top button on his pants, she actually wet her lips.

When he opened his fly and pulled out his cock, she almost swayed on her knees.

Marcus shoved his pants down farther. Then he said, "When this is over, I'm going to sleep beside you. I'm going to lie so damn close, you're going to feel every breath I take."

Jane didn't want to think about him descending upon her bed, not while she was desperate to pleasure him.

"Look all the way up," he told her.

She met his dark gaze.

He stared down at her and said, "Lick my balls. Rub your tongue all over them."

Her skin tingled. "Should I keep looking up while I'm doing it?"

"Yes. And I'm going to keep looking down at you."

She did exactly what was expected of her. She leaned forward, inhaled his wonderfully musky scent and lavished his balls, tasting each tender sac.

"Good. Now lick my cock."

No matter how demanding he was, she was more than willing to serve him. As she gripped the base of his shaft, he made a sound of approval. The way he was staring at her made her feel pretty damn sexy. Her big ugly T-shirt didn't matter anymore. She'd captured his dominant libido with a vengeance.

Doing what came naturally, she teased the tip of his penis with her tongue.

"More," he said.

She licked the entire length, getting him all wet.

He tunneled his hands in her hair. "Call me 'sir.'"

"Sir," she whispered.

"Say it louder."

"Sir."

Marcus tightened his hold on her hair, and she knew it was a physical warning that he was going to thrust into her mouth.

He went for it, and since she was ready for him, she took him hard and deep, showing him how deliberately subservient she could be.

He moved his hips, and she bobbed her head, helping him enjoy the experience.

Even as his cock jabbed the back of her throat, their gazes remained locked. She'd never given a blow job this powerful, but he was different from her other lovers.

Like the masochist she'd become, she pressed her knees against the floor, trying to create pain. She couldn't deny that she was as depraved as he was.

When her affair with him ended, would she go back to being normal? Or would she strip off her clothes and imagine herself in chains?

Shutting out her thoughts, Jane focused on giving him the best head of his life. He reacted by caressing her face. Roughly, gently, then roughly again, he traced the widely bowed shape of her lips, clearly excited by seeing his cock between them.

"When I come, you're going to swallow it," he said. "I'm going to fill up your mouth, and you're going to savor every drop."

It was an order she already intended to obey, but hearing him say it stirred a naughty ache between her legs.

She sucked harder, and as he got more aroused, the eye-to-eye connection grew stronger.

"You're fucking amazing," he said, his voice teetering between lust and affection.

Jane pushed him toward the madness, reveling in the signs of his pending ejaculation: the ragged pull of air into his lungs, the clenching of his abs.

Then, in the final moments, he resorted to tugging on her hair, separating it into two sections and using it like reins.

Would he whip her next time they were together?

Marcus thrust forward, and she braced herself for his release. He groaned low in his chest, and his milky fluid shot out.

In the silence that followed, they continued to stare at each other.

He stepped back and righted his pants. "I'm not going to dominate you any more tonight."

The salty taste of him remained on her tongue. "Then you're going home?"

"No. I'm sleeping in your bed. Beside you, like I said I would."

To her that still sounded like domination. "What if I told you to leave? Would you go this time?"

"Yes. Why? Do you want me to go?"

"No."

"Then why are we having this conversation?"

"I just wanted to check."

"Are you ready?"

To crawl under the covers with him? "I'm going to get some water first."

Jane went into the kitchen, and Marcus stayed in the living

room. Regardless, she remained within his eye range, and she could feel him watching her. She filled a glass from the refrigerator water dispenser and drank it.

After she returned to him, they went into her room, where her tousled bed looked as if she'd kicked her way out of it.

"Were you having a rough night before I showed up?"

She was still having a rough night. She wished that she hadn't enjoyed his punishment so dang much. Or that she wasn't anxiety ridden about allowing him to spend the night.

He pulled off his boots, then shed his socks. After he removed his trousers, he pinched the creases.

She asked, "Why are you so fussy with your clothes when you tossed mine around in the playroom before you chained me up?"

"Because you're the sub and I'm the dom." He placed his neatly folded pants on her dresser and got into bed. "And if I ever make you do domestic chores for me, you'll be prepared for how particular I am."

Domestic chores? "I should kick you out right now."

"Too late. I'm already settled in."

She frowned, and he squinted back at her, his dark eyes crinkling at the corners. She didn't question him about his removing his contact lenses. Obviously they were the kind that could be worn overnight; obviously he was protecting his mystique. She damned herself for thinking it was hot.

Jane didn't get undressed, and he didn't pressure her to get naked. He turned off the light and arranged their sleeping positions, putting his bared body right up against her clothed one. He put his arms around her, too.

Recalling what he'd said earlier about her feeling every breath he took, she squeezed her eyes shut.

But soon she relaxed and drifted off, oddly content in his arms.

Later that morning Jane awakened alone. She got up and searched the apartment, discovering that Marcus was gone. But he'd left a simple gift behind. On her computer desk was an origami heart he'd made from a piece of her inkjet paper.

She didn't know what to think, but she tucked the token away in a drawer for safekeeping.

Then she sat down and got online, looking for information about Marcus. But all she came across was his erotic hypnosis website, which she was already aware of, along with a few blogs and BDSM forums that mentioned his name. Everything was connected to his work. She didn't uncover anything that gave her more insight into the man behind the master.

Leaving her wondering who he really was.

Nine

On Suzanne's next date with Jake, he invited her to spend the night at his condo. Of course she readily agreed. She wanted to share his bed and get a feel for his home.

And what a home. Located in a resort-type setting, it catered to a luxurious lifestyle.

"This place is beautiful." She looked out the window and gazed through a scatter of palm trees, catching a moonlit glimpse of a tropical pool and hot tub. Was it any wonder he'd told her to bring her swimsuit? "Being a studio musician must be a lucrative job."

"It can be, depending on who you work for."

"You must work for some top artists."

He nodded, but he didn't name-drop.

In the silence, she considered the songs he kept to himself. Would he ever have the desire to share them with the world? Another curious thought crossed her mind. Did he write about his lovers in his erotic-themed songs? Would he ever use her name in one of them?

"Can I get you something?" he asked.

"I'm sorry. What?"

"Soda, beer, wine, hard lemonade?"

"Hard lemonade sounds good."

He got it from the mini fridge in his portable bar, along with a beer for himself. Then he reached behind the counter and removed a small gold box with a shiny ribbon.

He extended it. "Just a little something."

Surprised, she removed the ribbon and opened the box. Inside was a slim black container that looked suspiciously like a tube of lipstick. She lifted the cap and discovered that the luscious pink lip color was a soft jelly vibrator.

Jake said, "Cool, huh? You can carry it around in your purse without anyone knowing what it is."

It was rather cool: a sexy device between lovers. She hoped that he would write a song about her someday. She wanted to be someone who inspired him.

"Do you like it?" he asked.

"Oh, yes, thank you. We can do fun things with this."

"Totally fun, anytime and anywhere." He kissed her hotly on

the mouth. "Next time we go out to eat, you can slip it under your skirt and give yourself a nice little buzz."

She put the vibrator in her purse, next to her real lipstick. "You're wicked, Jake."

"After we finish our drinks, we can kick back in the Jacuzzi." He nipped her earlobe. "And I can put my hands inside your swimsuit if there's no one around."

"I thought you liked other people being around."

"I do. But tonight I want to play privately. Or as privately as we can in an open area."

"I'm game." To be wild and free and imagine him honoring her in a song.

He grinned and clanked his bottle against hers, toasting their hot tub tryst.

About ten minutes later, he put on board shorts and Suzanne climbed into a sassy little bikini. He grabbed two big beach towels and they went out to the pool area, which luckily they had to themselves.

They sat in the hot tub, the water bubbling around them. "This is my favorite place to relax," he said.

"I can see why. It's therapeutic."

"Sometimes it gets noisy during the day. There aren't any kids who live here, but a few of my neighbors are divorced dads, and they bring their rug rats over. On weekends, they band together in the pool."

"Does that annoy you?"

"Not at all. When I'm in the mood to goof around, I hang out with them."

Suzanne couldn't be more surprised. "You like kids?"

"Sure. Besides, I'm a kick-ass Marco Polo player."

She couldn't help but ask, "Do you think you'll ever settle down and have a family?"

"Me? Are you serious?" He gave his head a quick and jerky shake. "I wouldn't take my Marco Polo skills that far."

"I plan on having a husband and kids someday. I keep hoping to find the right guy."

He made a face. "Don't be looking in my direction."

Damn, but his remark stung. Was it because she was having fantasies about becoming his muse? Or were her secret longings developing into something more? God, she hoped not.

He moved closer, and an awkward silence rose between them. But before it got thicker, he cut through the discomfort, keeping his promise about putting his hand inside her swimsuit. He started with her bikini top, sneaking in to rub one of her nipples and bring it to a peak.

She turned to face him, and they kissed. His mouth tasted cool amid the hot, hot water. He tugged her closer and caressed her other nipple.

Suzanne sighed. He was getting hard beneath his shorts, his cock bulging against the fabric. But no matter how aroused either of them got, they weren't going to fuck.

Jake as much as said so. "This is the best kind of foreplay. Playing around like teenagers who aren't ready to go all the way."

She rubbed herself between his legs. "When are we going to be ready?"

"When we're in bed, like normal people."

That made her smile. "We're far from normal."

"We can pretend." He snaked his hand down, nudging her away from his cock.

"You're not playing fair." But when he pushed the same hand down the front of her bikini bottoms and cupped her mound, she changed her mind.

"I like that your pussy is waxed," he said.

"You're smooth, too." She recalled how it felt to stroke him at the restaurant, to bring him dangerously close to an orgasm. "Did you jerk off that night after you got home like you said you would?"

"Yes, ma'am. I did it in my bed, and I got the sheets all sticky. The same sheets we're going to sleep on tonight." He worked a finger over the hood of her clit and made the little gem pop out. "But I washed them after I was done."

Damn, he was dirty, talking about laundering come-stained linens while the Jacuzzi jets propelled water at her. "I remember the fantasy you told me."

"About you kneeling over my face?"

Her skin quavered; her cunt vibrated. He was rubbing her clit in earnest. "Yes."

"Do you want to live out that fantasy tonight? Right before I fuck you senseless?"

She nodded and pitched forward to put her arms around his neck. He kept doing delicious things with the hand that was inside her bikini bottoms.

"Are you going to come for me, Susie Q?"

"When I'm kneeling over your face? You know I will."

He kept working his magic. "How about right now?"

She moaned lightly, the pleasured sound drifting into the night. From the moment they first met, he knew how to drive her sweetly mad.

And that was exactly what he did. While she closed her eyes, he brought her to a powerful climax.

After they returned to the house, they peeled off their swimsuits and reclined on Jake's bed. But they left the next phase of foreplay for later. For now, they started talking, almost like a real couple.

He leaned on his elbow. "You're different than I thought you were."

She didn't ponder what he meant. "Because I want a husband and kids?"

He nodded. "I wouldn't have pegged Susie Q for Suzy Homemaker."

She couldn't very well disagree with his cleverly worded observation. "I know I don't seem like that type. But I'm a product of
my environment."

"How so?"

"I had a crappy childhood, and I promised myself when I was
growing up that I'd create my own family someday. A happy,
healthy, normal one, like the kind I used to see on TV."

"I'm a product of my rotten environment, too. But all it inspired
was the need to escape."

"So you ran away and hit the streets?"

"Yep."

"Maybe we should compare our crappy childhoods," she said,
half serious and half joking.

He responded in the same tone. "Compare them for what? A
prize? I'd win."

"You can't be sure of that. I might've had a drug-addicted
mom. Or a—" She stopped talking. She'd caught his attention,
and she'd caught it hard.

"Was your mom an addict?" he asked.

She nodded. "Prescription drugs. But that still counts."

"Mine was a crackhead."

A beat of pain passed between them.

"Did yours ever get clean?" he asked.

She shook her head. "She refused to recognize that she had
a problem. She was self-indulgent when I was growing up and

she still is. I was the 'mistake' who ruined her figure and her youth."

"That's harsh. What about your dad? How does he fit into the equation?"

"They got divorced when I was ten, and he remarried and moved out of state. He paid child support and did what the courts expected him to do, but I hardly ever saw him. What about you?"

"I've never met my dad, and my mom didn't have a maternal bone in her body. She didn't concern herself with putting food on the table. She didn't cover me with a blanket when I was cold or bandage my knees when I fell down. She never did anything except call me the bastard child of Beelzebub. When I was little, I actually thought that was my old man's name."

"Where did she come up with Beelzebub?"

"She heard it from some old guy in the neighborhood who used to preach at the druggies. Beelzebub is sometimes used as another name for Satan." He went on to say, "But the old guy used to talk about angels, too, the warring kind with armor, steel swords, and big powerful wings. To get back at my mom, I used to imagine them in my mind, kicking Satan's ass." He shrugged. "And now I'm a musician with phony black eyes who pretends to be a fallen angel at a club. I'm not sure who has the last laugh about that one."

None of it was funny, but she understood what he meant. "I'm sorry you had such a lousy childhood, Jake."

"You, too."

"I think yours was worse. At least my mom used to fix dinner and do all the seemingly normal stuff."

"So I get the prize?"

"Yes."

"Then put your clothes back on, Suzanne."

She started. "What?"

"That'll be my prize."

Confused, she gave him a blank stare.

"The fantasy," he clarified. "Don't you remember how I described it when we talked about it at the restaurant?"

Ah, yes. She recited the details. "I was taking off my panties and hiking up my dress, then I was kneeling over your face and moving closer, showing you my clit."

"Your swollen little clit," he provided, verbatim.

She smiled. "I'll go get my clothes on." It wasn't the same dress or panties she'd worn on the night he conjured the fantasy, but the principle was same.

She went into his bathroom where she'd left her clothes. Her damp bikini was there, as well, hanging over the shower rail by its string ties. Jake's board shorts were looped over the faucet in the tub.

Caught up in the atmosphere, she imagined herself living with him: sharing the master bathroom, cuddling in bed, eating at the same table, splashing in the pool with his divorced neighbor's kids. Then what was she going to do? Marry him and raise a family?

She put on her clothes and scolded herself. He'd already warned her not to view him in that manner and she knew better than to think along those lines.

So what in the world was she doing?

Before she got more conflicted, she quieted her emotions and returned to Jake.

She rejoined him in bed, and he watched her with anticipation. He didn't say anything, and she took that to mean that he wasn't going to give her further direction. But she already knew what she was supposed to do.

Beginning the naughty game, she reached under her dress and peeled off her panties. Getting into the agreed-upon position, she crawled over his face and bunched her hem, pulling it up past her thighs.

With her heart in her throat, she glanced down to get his reaction. He stared back at her, and with the way his head was tipped, she could see the strong column of his neck and the slight bob of his Adam's apple. He looked hungry as hell.

Suzanne widened her knee stance and got closer. Soon she would be sitting on his face and rubbing back and forth.

But first . . .

She lifted her dress higher. While holding it with her left hand, she used her right hand to put her fingers between her legs. Then, eager for the final enticement, she opened her nether lips and she showed him her clit, a delicate pink nub desperate for his attention.

He finally spoke, his voice vibrating from his chest. "You're beautiful. All of you. So damn beautiful."

Loving the way his compliment made her feel, she let him look at her a bit longer. She knew that this wasn't intended to be a romantic act, but intimacy between them almost made it seem that way.

Ready for his touch, she got low enough for him to use his tongue, and he teased her with soft circles and gentle strokes. Suzanne sighed, and he reached up and caressed her butt cheeks. But his dreamy seduction only lasted long enough for her to catch her breath.

Within no time, he cupped her ass with strong, hard fingers and tasted her with a vengeance. Suzanne dived into the rhythm and arched her body. He was putting his mouth all over her, creating carnal sensations.

Slick and wet. Sweet and dirty.

Like the sexually instinctive man he was, he did everything exactly the way she liked it. He licked her labia like it was his favorite flavor of ice cream. He sucked on her clit. He encouraged her to moan and thrash and rotate her hips.

She wanted it to last, to go on and on, but no matter how hard she tried, she couldn't stop the inferno that burst through her loins and ignited her veins.

Suzanne bucked wildly against him, and in the midst of the final shudder, he rolled her onto her back, peeled off her dress and nudged her legs apart.

He grappled for a condom in a valet tray beside the bed, and when he looked at her with those purposely dark eyes, she feared that was she on the verge of falling for him.

To combat the feeling, she clawed his back when he entered her, reminding herself that this was an affair and nothing more.

At the break of dawn, Suzanne got out of Jake's bed, where he was still asleep.

After padding into the bathroom to splash some cool water on her face, she slipped on a silky robe she'd brought with her and went into the living room.

She walked over to the window and gazed out at the tropical view. She wasn't used to the quiet. Even at this hour, there would be activity in her apartment building with people starting their cars or going outside to jog.

Settling into the silence, she turned toward the bookcase in the corner. She might as well find something to read. Going back to sleep would be impossible. Once Suzanne was up, she was up.

She scanned Jake's books. Mostly they were music tech stuff. She kept searching for something that would interest her, then she noticed two cloth-covered books that looked like journals.

Was this where Jake kept his songs?

She opened the first one. Sure enough it contained handwritten lyrics. She knew it was invasive to read them, but it wasn't as if he'd put them under lock and key. Besides, all she was going to do was take a quick peek.

Suzanne's quick peek turned into a full reading venture. She couldn't help being enthralled with his work. He'd definitely penned some carnal stuff, but it didn't seem to be influenced by any of his lovers, at least not in a specific way. Now more than ever she wanted to be his muse.

The book wasn't completely full. There were still blank pages waiting for new creations. Imagining her name in it, she put it back on the shelf.

The second book, she assumed, contained his good versus evil lyrics. Curious, she glanced at the first song, but the words blurred before her eyes. Squinting to clear her vision, she looked at it again.

The word "demon" appeared on the page followed by "wrath." In the next instant, they were gone. Not blurred. But gone.

Had he used some sort of invisible ink?

She studied it once more. This time the word "angel" lit up the page. Not figuratively. But literally. It actually sparkled, as bright and shiny as silver glitter.

He must have used something to create these effects. Whatever it was, Suzanne couldn't let go. She wanted to see more, to read more. But the page went blank again.

Much too curious, she ran her hand along the paper. "Angel" came back, and it was warm and comforting beneath her fingers.

How was any of this possible?

She thought about the angels Jake had mentioned last night. The figments of his youthful imagination that were kicking Satan's ass.

She closed her eyes for a second and a magical sensation engulfed her. Beautiful magic. Her body turned cold. Dark magic. Confused and frightened, she opened her eyes.

Pain . . . pain . . . pain was scribbled all over the page.

Suzanne dropped the book and the horrible scribble went away.

Taking a chance, she picked it up again and felt an emotional connection to Jake. Then she turned and saw him standing there.

In the next crazy instant, all of the words reappeared and flew off the page, twirling in front of both of them like a mini tornado. Good words, bad words, good feelings, bad feelings.

"Oh, Christ," he muttered. He seemed as startled as she was.

"What's going on?" she asked, afraid to move.

"I don't know."

"You have to know something. It's your song."

"I don't want to talk about it."

Was he fucking kidding? "You'd better say something or I don't think this is going to stop." She pressured him for answers. "What's the song about?"

"Something we did when we were on the streets."

"We? You mean you and Marcus and Damien?"

"Yes, but the lyrics are just bits and pieces. I didn't define the whole experience. I would've never put all of it down on paper. We promised each other that we would keep the details a secret."

The tornado spun faster. "Did it involve magic?"

"We cast some spells that we shouldn't have."

The words returned to the book and Suzanne snapped it closed. He came forward and pried it from her fingers.

He shoved it back into the bookcase, and she assumed that his heart was beating as erratically as hers.

"Did you mess with demonic stuff?" she asked.

"Yes."

"And angel stuff, too?"

He nodded, then went over to the bar and poured himself a shot of whiskey. "Do you want one?"

She shook her head. No matter how frazzled she was, she couldn't drink at this hour.

He belted it down. "You shouldn't have read my work. You should have respected my privacy."

"I know. I'm sorry." She glanced at the bookcase. "But it's a little late to reprimand me, considering." She plopped onto the sofa. "I guess it's safe to assume that your songs haven't done anything like that before?"

He sat next to her. "No. Never."

After they calmed down a bit, he said, "I need to talk to Marcus and Damien about this. I need them to help me figure out why this happened. You should go home, and I'll call you later and fill you in."

"Okay." She wanted to talk to her friends, too. She suspected that Emily was going to freak out. But at this point, she couldn't blame her. Something bizarre was going on.

And Suzanne was smack-dab in the middle of it.

Ten

Suzanne waited anxiously to hear from Jake, with Emily and Jane by her side. As predicted, Emily had freaked out. Jane kept calm, almost eerily so, intensifying the moment.

"You believe me, don't you?" Suzanne asked her.

"Yes, but only because I know you're not the type to imagine things."

Emily jumped in. "What's that supposed to mean? That I *am* the type? That if this would have happened to me, you would've thought I was hallucinating?"

Jane patted Auntie Em's knee. "No, that's not what I meant. I'm just trying to wrap my mind around the fact that magic exists. On the night I couldn't sleep and Marcus showed up at my apartment, I was fighting a case of the heebie-jeebies, which is totally out of character for me. And now Suzanne has had a *truly* weird experience."

"I knew there was something demonic going on," Emily said.

Suzanne replied, "But there were good and bad feelings attached to the song. Wouldn't something demonic be all bad?"

Emily seemed confused. "Maybe it was a trick."

"When it was happening, I could feel the magic, and afterward I could tell that Jake was telling the truth. That they'd cast some spells when they were younger and it involved both angels and demons." Suzanne blew out a breath. "I just wish he would hurry and call. But when he does I'm taking the phone outside."

Emily frowned. "Why?"

"Because having you and Jane hovering in the background will make me more nervous than I already am. But I promise I won't leave anything out. I'll tell you everything he says."

Jane interjected, "I agree that you should have a private conversation with him. You don't need to be distracted."

About ten minutes later, Suzanne's cell phone chimed, and she rushed onto her concrete patio to answer it.

Jake came on the line, and said, "It's me, Susie Q."

"I know. I saw your name on the screen. Did your friends help you figure anything out?"

"They think the song manifested into magic because of my guilt."

"What guilt?"

"I'm the one who came up with the idea to cast spells when we were younger, and I've had a hard time letting it go. That's why I write those types of songs. They're my outlet."

"That doesn't explain why the song acted up in front of me."

"Actually, Marcus has a theory about that. He thinks that you're getting emotionally attached to me, so the magic attached itself to you, too. But I told him that you weren't developing feelings for me." A frown sounded in his voice. "You're not, are you?"

"No," she lied.

"Good. Because what I said last night was true. I don't have an interest in settling down, and I'm not the right guy for you."

"I never thought that you were." She'd been warning herself not to fall for him, and this cinched it. No more longing to be his muse. No more romantic fantasies.

After a second of silence, Jake said, "Damien wants to tell Emily what transpired during those spells. He thinks it will make her feel better if she knows the truth and it comes from him."

"He's willing to part with the details? How do you and Marcus feel about that?"

"Marcus thinks it's a good idea."

"But you don't?"

"Truthfully, I'm still unnerved that my lyrics turned to magic in front of you. But there isn't much I can do about it now. It's a bit late to pretend that you and your friends aren't being pulled into this because of me and a song I probably should've never written."

Emily agreed to meet Damien in a public place, so she gave him directions to a park near her house. And now they sat on a picnic bench in the sun, with green grass surrounding them.

She was beyond nervous, and she was just as attracted to him as she was from the moment they'd first exchanged glances at the club.

He said, "Are you ready to hear the secret we've been keeping?"

"Yes," she responded, hoping that he was embarking on the absolute truth.

"As you know, we were runaways who met on the streets, and we were having a tough time of it."

"How old were you?"

"All of us were seventeen. Young enough to be afraid, but old enough that no one really cared. We were scrounging to eat, trying to find places to sleep, butting heads with gangbangers, getting beat up and robbed."

When Emily was seventeen, she was going to school dances and preparing for college.

Jake came up with an idea to use magic to protect us, and we got a hold of a spell that was supposed to conjure a guardian. An angel," he clarified. "A winged warrior who wore gilded armor and carried a steel sword. Those were Jake's favorite kinds of angels."

Engrossed in his story, she scooted to the edge of her seat.

He continued, "The spell didn't work, and we got angry and confused. Things were getting worse out there, and we didn't have the kinds of homes we could go back to."

"So you turned to dark magic?"

"We were desperate, and we thought that if we invoked a demon, it would provide the power and strength we needed. Jake was especially convinced that it would work. By then, he was fed up with his belief in angels."

She folded her arms, warding off a chill. "What happened?"

"We cast the spell, and a demon appeared." His voice went rough. "But it's dead now."

She could do little more than stare.

"One of us killed it," he said. "But which of us it was or how the creature was slain isn't important. That's a detail we'd rather not share."

Emily continued to stare at him. His hair was blowing softly in the breeze, and in the daylight, his eyes looked even blacker.

As if he'd caught a glimpse of her thought, he said, "We didn't start wearing contact lenses as a gimmick. When the demon appeared, it created trauma to our eyes. Not in how we see, but in how our eyes look. The pigment in our irises is messed up."

She was still stunned into silence, still trying to envision one of them killing a demon. Could a teenage boy actually destroy a demon? Emily mulled it over. Anything was possible, wasn't it? As long as faith and prayer were involved?

He went on about their eyes. "In the beginning, we all wore sunglasses so no one would know. Then we switched to contacts. Black is the only shade that masks the damage. Contacts require a prescription in the United States, so we've always gotten ours from an outside source. We couldn't very well go to an eye doctor and explain what happened to our eyes."

She finally spoke. "I didn't believe the story about the gimmick."

"Do you believe everything I'm telling you now?"

"Yes." Heaven help her, she did. But it left a disturbing question in her mind. She inhaled a sharp breath. "I don't understand why, after what you and your friends have been through, you would choose demons for your identities at the club."

"The experience created darkness in us that we're still fighting. Before the demon was killed, it . . ."

Her pulse jumped. "It what?"

"Tortured us."

"Oh, my God. I'm so sorry."

"Jake felt it the worst. I didn't think he was going to survive it."

Needing to touch him, she reached across the tabletop for his hand. Was Damien the boy who'd killed the demon? Who'd ended the torture?

"I'm going to tell Jane and Suzanne about all of this when I get back," she said.

"Yes, I imagine that they're waiting to hear." His fingers locked with hers. "Will you come to my house afterward? Will you stay with me tonight?"

She nodded, unable to deny him. Or herself.

Damien's house, a white bungalow with brick detail, was located in Laurel Canyon and surrounded by mature trees and leafy plants.

The living room presented vaulted ceilings, French windows, and furniture from different eras. His paintings were displayed in prominent places. In a watercolor behind the sofa, a delicate woman, draped in a glittering wedding gown and carrying a bouquet of pink flowers, stood on the steps of a dilapidated chapel. The tall, trim groom waiting at the crumbling altar wore a crisp tuxedo and grotesque mask.

Emily didn't comment on the man's distorted features. But what could she say? Damien's artwork was a reflection of the darkness that he and his friends were fighting.

He gave her a tour of the rest of the house. Built in the 1930s, it had two bedrooms and one bathroom. The room he used as his studio was cluttered with shelves and wooden easels. She imagined him working at all hours, unleashing the creative fury that drove him.

While they were in his bedroom, he placed her bag beside a Victorian dresser.

The bed, she noticed, was draped with a lavish Moroccan-style quilt. To keep her heart steady, she glanced away from it. That was the bed that would seal their salacious union, where he'd promised to make her come.

"Are you hungry?" he asked.

She shifted her gaze back to him. Did he mean for food?

"I can prepare a snack. Wine, bread, cheese."

"That sounds good."

They left his bedroom, and he offered her a chair at the dining room table. She couldn't see him from where she sat, but she could hear him moving about in the kitchen. While she waited, she glanced at the backyard, which was rich in foliage and seasoned with a canyon view.

Soon Damien appeared with their snack. Along with the bread, he'd provided bite-sized pieces of cheddar and Gouda. He placed two silver goblets on the table, too.

She peered into hers. The liquid was bloodred. She looked up at him. "My church uses a silver chalice as a communion cup."

He sat across from her. "Then why are you apprehensive to drink from that one?"

"I'm not." She peered at the dark liquid again. "What kind of wine is it?"

"A California merlot." He sipped from his.

She allowed herself a small sip, as well. She wasn't a wine connoisseur, but she detected a note of blackberry. "It's good."

They ate in silence for a short while, then he asked, "What did Jane and Suzanne say when you told them about the details of the spell?"

"They wouldn't have believed a story like that in the past, but after what happened to Suzanne at Jake's house, they're aware that magic exists. So they're doing their best to come to terms with it."

"It's good that everyone knows the truth and we can move on." He changed the subject. "So, what do you do to keep busy when you're not working?"

"I like to cook. I garden, too."

"What do you grow?"

"Mostly herbs. My late grandmother taught me about them." She spoke candidly, letting him know how cautious Grandma had been. "She didn't grow devil's claw, though."

"Devil's claw isn't dangerous."

"I know. It was the name that troubled her."

"Some say that belladonna is the devil's herb. It's poisonous when it's used incorrectly."

"Grandma didn't grow poisonous herbs."

"What about oregano?"

"That's not poisonous."

"I wasn't inferring that it was. In medieval Europe, people

used to carry oregano with them as protection from witches, water sprites, and demons. The smoke from a burning plant was supposed to prevent the devil from aiding his servants here on earth."

Emily thought about the oregano that flourished on her patio. She hadn't known its history.

Damien said, "Valerian was used to protect against evil spirits, too. They also believed that it was an aphrodisiac. That when it was mixed with wine, it could turn even the most virtuous woman lustful."

She closed her fingers around the stem of her chalice. "Did you put some in my wine?"

He frowned. "You still don't trust me."

"I'm just nervous."

"I didn't put anything in your wine. I'd never do that. Besides, I want your attraction to me to be natural. Not something created from an aphrodisiac."

"You're all I've been thinking about."

"Even when you were resisting me?"

"Yes."

He stood up and extended his hand. "Then come to my room, Emily. Let's be together now."

This was the defining moment. She got out of her chair and moved toward him. They went to his bedroom, and he closed the blinds. Dusk had begun to settle, bringing shadows with it.

He removed three white votives from a shelf and placed them on top of the dresser. "I think women look beautiful by candlelight." He sparked a match and lit each one. "And you're the most beautiful woman who's ever crossed my path."

He reached for her, and they kissed. Moments later, she stepped out of her shoes, and he lowered the straps on her dress. Little by little, her clothes fell by the wayside, while he remained fully covered.

"Your turn," she told him.

He shook his head. "First I want you to lie on my bed in the way we talked about, with your hair fanned across my pillow and your legs spread."

Lord help her, she wanted that, too.

He turned down the quilt, and she got in bed and put her head on a pillow. He came over and arranged her hair, threading it through his fingers before he released it.

Emily felt as if she were posing for a painting, a nude that would be captured in the softest of colors. But there was no canvas, no brushes, and no tubes of acrylic. If the artist was painting her, he was doing it in his mind.

He stepped back. "I could look at you forever."

She went blushingly shy. By now, her legs were open and her vulva was exposed.

As silence drifted between them, he removed his clothes. He unbuttoned his shirt and parted the billowy fabric. When he cast it aside, it floated poetically to the floor. His slim-fitting trousers came next. He peeled them off quickly and efficiently, stripping down to a pair of boxer briefs.

Although he was marvelously toned, she didn't picture him working out at a gym. She envisioned him using the environment in which he lived to strengthen his body, running through the canyon at reclusive hours, his feet pounding the earth.

He discarded his underwear, and she gazed at the most intimate part of him. He was already half aroused, his balls taut between his legs, and his penis jutting toward his navel. It embarrassed her that she was staring at him as if she'd never seen a naked man before. But his beauty overwhelmed her.

He got into bed, and they turned to face each other.

"Show me how you like to be touched," he said.

She caught her breath. He wanted her to pleasure herself in front of him?

He persisted. "If you show me, I'll know exactly how to make you come."

No man had ever cared so much about giving her an orgasm, and that made being seduced by him wildly romantic. But it made her self-conscious, too.

"Do it, Emily."

"I usually do it with my eyes closed."

"Then close your eyes."

"But I don't lie on my side like this."

"Then get into whatever position feels right to you."

"With you watching?"

"You won't see me if your eyes are closed."

"I'll feel you being there."

"That's part of what will draw us closer together, of what this is about."

He kissed her softly on the lips. Steeped in surrender, she agreed to his request.

As she rolled onto her back and closed her eyes, she became more aware of her surroundings: the smell of burning wax, the luxurious texture of the sheets, the sound of her own erratic breathing. Of course she was aware of Damien, too, just as she knew she would be.

Since it was impossible to pretend that she wasn't being watched, she didn't even try. Instead, she tightened her rear and lifted her hips, pressing the tips of her fingers against her clit. Normally she would fantasize about a dream lover, but he was already there.

While she rubbed in tiny circles, he said, "We're going to be together as often as we can, and we're going to do all sorts of sensual things."

She kept her eyes closed, encouraging him to feed the fantasy, "Like what?"

"We'll use the herbs you grow to make massage oil."

Emily sighed. "Peppermint, lavender, lemon balm, and sage."

"And rose petals and yarrow. I have those plants in my yard."

She pictured his foliage-laden property with its twisting vines and flowering perennials.

"We'll cook decadent meals, too," he told her. "Foods rich in creams and sauces."

"Will we make love in your kitchen?"

"Yes."

Feeling uncharacteristically free, she rubbed herself a little harder, a little faster. "Will we fuck there, too?"

"As often as you want." He spoke directly into her ear. "We'll do it against the countertops. On the floor. I'll fuck you so hard and deep, you'll want to scream."

Moaning low in her throat, she slid her fingers lower and pushed them inside. While she thrust in and out, she rocked her hips and pressed her thumb against her clit.

He continued, "We'll do anything that makes us feel good. We'll use my bathtub like a vat and pour wine all over each other. We'll take turns licking it off."

Emily got wet. Really, really wet.

Wanting to see Damien, she opened her eyes. Their gazes met and held, increasing the sexual energy. Curious, she glanced lower. Light and shadow played upon his naked body, accentuating his leanly sculpted muscles and showcasing his fully erect cock.

He said, "Put your fingers in my mouth."

Oh, hot heaven. He wanted her to feed him her creamy flavor? He was downright sinful.

She offered him her fingers, and he sucked lustfully on each one. Afterward, he got between her legs and kissed her down there.

Normally she didn't like having a man's face pressed between her thighs. Normally she was too timid to relax. But when Damien told her to put her legs on his shoulders and scoot closer, she followed his lead, much too eager to give herself to him.

He excited her in ways she'd never imagined. One minute he was amazingly gentle and in the next he was licking her with masculine fury. Back and forth he went, making her arch and flex.

She rotated her hips, chanting his name in her mind.

Damien. Beautiful Damien.

It was too late to make him stop. Her juices were already flowing into his mouth. She was already starting to shudder, to moan, to come . . .

The orgasm slammed into her, exploding into a prism of volcanic heat and spinning colors, like paint splattering from a melting palette.

Struggling to recover, she lowered her legs from his shoulders, and although her luxury-wracked body went limp, tiny spasms and honey-slick sensations lingered.

He studied her. "Are you all right?"

She caught her breath and nodded.

"I can hold you if you need to rest."

She nearly shattered. She was barely holding on by a God-save-me thread. "I don't want to rest. I want you inside me."

He reached into the nightstand drawer and removed a condom. He was already hard, so all he had to do was open the packet and put it on.

She watched him, desperate to feel the weight of his body pressing down on hers and wishing the craving would subside.

Damien entered her, creating a rhythm that sent shards of electricity through her blood.

"I shouldn't need you this badly," she said.

"We need each other, and I'm going to make you come again."

Twice in the same day? She couldn't even do that to herself. "I'm not multiorgasmic."

"You will be when I'm done with you."

"When are you going to be done with me? For good, I mean."

"Not for a long time. Maybe never."

He lowered his head to kiss her, and she imagined how they looked, tangled in each other's limbs. She glided a hand down his chest and along the flatness of his stomach, absorbing the warmth of skin. She skimmed the patch of hair that surrounded his penis, too.

They kissed and kissed, until he got the urge to change positions. "Turn over, Emily. Let me have you the way an animal would have its mate."

She climbed onto her hands and knees, and he got behind her and grasped her hips. When she felt him reenter her, she moaned.

He said, "You know what else we're going to do together? I'm going to spend hours painting your body. I'm going to turn you into my canvas." He reached around to caress her clit. "And you're going to be my most erotic work of art."

Reacting to his words, to the strum of his fingers, to the

stroking motion of his cock, she pushed back against him. He hissed in her ear, and the penetration got deeper and wilder, his balls slapping her butt.

Emily couldn't combat the fire. She clawed the sheet and another orgasm slammed through her. Damien came, too, and even after he withdrew, she still felt connected to him.

Totally and completely enraptured.

Eleven

Emily blinked into the tiny of slats of sunlight creeping through the closed blinds. Then she rolled over and glanced at Damien. He was still asleep, his hair waving haphazardly across his forehead. Although she was tempted to smooth it from his brow, she kept her hands to herself.

She gazed at his magnificently formed body. The sheet covered him from the waist down, but she knew what he looked like below the silky drape. She knew what it felt like to make love with him, too.

He opened his eyes, and they stared at each other. He leaned over to kiss her, and she realized that no matter how close they'd gotten last night, they were still strangers.

"I don't even know your last name," she said.

"It's Black."

Like the color of the lenses that masked his damaged eyes? That compelled her to ask, "Is it your real name?"

"No. After the demon was slain, all of us changed our names. We needed to start over."

An uncomfortable feeling came over her. What if the demon had some sort of hold over the one who'd killed it? What if before it died, its spirit entered the boy's body?

Damien kissed her again, and she fought a shiver.

"What's wrong?" he asked.

"I'm just a little cold."

He brought the blanket up around them. "Better?"

Distracted by her troubled thoughts, she nodded absently. If a possession had taken place, then that would make the rumors true. Damien or one of his friends would qualify as being a demon.

"You still seem chilled," he said.

"It's just the morning air." She flattened her palm against his chest. If he had a creature inside him, would she be able to feel it?

His heartbeat stirred softly beneath her touch, making the moment confusingly romantic. How could she be worried about a possession when he seemed so warm and gentle? She needed to stop letting her superstitions run away with her.

"Let's make breakfast," he said. "You can wear my robe if you'd like."

They got out of bed and he went to the closet and brought back a lightweight robe that looked like a kimono of some sort.

He helped her put it on, and she said, "This is beautiful."

"I got it downtown in Little Tokyo. But I've been to Japan. I've been just about everywhere." He took a pair of boxer briefs out of his dresser, slipped them on, then climbed into a pair of holey jeans. "I like to immerse myself in the sexual culture of other countries."

"I haven't been out of the States. But I plan to travel when I can afford it. For the history and regular culture." She watched him zip his jeans. "Not anything sexual."

He roamed his gaze over her. "Being with me is going to change you."

She was well aware of his erotic impact on her. After a few anxious breaths, she said, "I need to freshen up a bit before we start the meal."

"Me, too. But you can go first if you want privacy."

"Thank you."

They took turns in the lone bathroom, then met up in the kitchen, a room with gray granite countertops, colorful Spanish-tiled floors, and a stainless-steel fridge.

"Do you want coffee or tea?" Damien asked.

"I drink tea."

"So do I. The coffee is for guests."

Wondering about who visited him, she asked, "Other women from Aeonian?"

"I prefer to keep groupie activity limited to the club."

"You extended an invitation to me right away, and we met at the club."

"You're not a groupie." He put water on to boil, using a bright yellow teakettle.

She pressed him for more information. "Girlfriends, then?"

"I've had countless lovers, but I rarely bring anyone to my home, and when I do, it doesn't last beyond a night or two." He turned to face her. "No one has ever interested me enough for a relationship. No one has ever triggered that kind of need."

Emily thought about what he'd said last night about intending to keep her for as long as he possibly could. He seemed to be thinking about it, too.

Before she got trapped in a discussion of her own making, she redirected his focus. "We should get started on breakfast."

Damien suggested pesto-scrambled eggs, mushroom and cheese potatoes, maple bacon strips, and chocolate and strawberry waffles, verifying how passionately he lived his life.

The teakettle whistled, and they drank a spicy blend chai while they gathered the ingredients.

During the cooking process, he rubbed up against her whenever the mood struck him, reminding her that they'd talked about having sex in the kitchen.

He refreshed their tea, and they sat down to eat, their chairs side by side. Halfway through the richly seasoned meal, he leaned over and kissed her. Then he removed her borrowed robe and pulled her onto his lap. He took the chocolate sauce intended for the waffles, squeezed the bottle and drizzled it down the front of her naked body.

The sticky substance trailed between her breasts and pooled at her navel. He kissed her again, and as his tongue tangled with hers, she flung her arms around his neck, making his skin sticky, too.

While their mouths were still fused, she heard plates, cups, and silverware rattle. Was he pushing them out of the way to make room for her? Yes, he was. Ending the kiss, he lifted her up and placed her on the edge of the table, directly in front of him. Somehow he'd managed not to spill anything, not even the tea. But that didn't stop him from creating sexy havoc.

He opened her legs, and although he didn't pour the chocolate sauce on her pussy, he smeared it on her thighs and began the sensual process of licking it off.

Emily indulged in the sauce, too. She used her fingers to taste the sweetness from her nipples. She even sampled it from her belly button.

He said, "I'm going to fuck you when we're done feasting."

Her hunger whirred. This was the best breakfast she'd ever had. Now she understood the concept of food play.

Bohemian as ever, he flashed his one-dimpled smile. He had chocolate all over his lips. But soon he wiped his mouth with a napkin and sponged off her body with one of the leftover waffles. He gave her a waffle to sop up the messiness on his chest and stomach, too. But no matter how many waffles they used, a residue remained. He went over to the sink and came back with warm wet cloths, and they did the job right. "Feel good?" he asked, as he bathed her thighs and teased her center.

"More than good." Emily wanted him to fuck her so badly, she could've screamed. But him making her scream was part of the discussion they'd had last night.

He motioned to a canister on the counter. "What do you think is in there?"

"It looks like a cookie jar." But somehow she doubted that was what it was.

He brought the canister over to the table and told her to open it. She lifted the lid and saw that it was filled with brightly colored condom packages.

"Pick one," he said.

Excited by the contents, she chose a textured style. They didn't need a lubricated one; she was already wet.

He undid his jeans and pushed down his boxers. His cock sprang free, and Emily opened the packet and sheathed him.

He pulled her to the edge of the table and thrust hotly into her. Greedy for more, she wrapped her legs around him, taking him deeper.

"Let's get messy again," he said. "Let's fuck nice and dirty."

Clean. Dirty. Crazy.

She was game for anything. Good thing, too. While he pounded into her, he went wild with the chocolate. He even grabbed handfuls of scrambled egg and potato and added that to the mix. They kissed and drove each other to the brink of food-play madness.

Caught in a delicious frenzy, she thrashed in his arms and breathed desperately against his neck. When she came, all she could think was how much she loved being his lover.

Hours later, freshly showered and still thoroughly consumed with him, she got ready to go home.

On her way out the door, she glanced over at the painting behind the sofa. The bride at the dilapidated chapel remained still, but the grotesquely masked groom turned his head and looked right at Emily, as if he was confirming her suspicion from earlier.

That the demon's spirit was still alive.

After a grueling day of juggling multiple writing projects and hardly getting anything done, Jane sat on her sofa, with Suzanne perched at her side. Focusing on every word being spoken, they listened to Emily panic about a painting that had moved in her presence.

She'd already explained that she'd gotten a "feeling" that a possession had taken place when the demon had been killed, and then later, the groom had made eye contact with her. Jane wasn't sure that it was absolute proof of a possession, but she wasn't going to dismiss the possibility, either. After all of these strange occurrences, she was keeping a very open mind.

"Was Damien with you when it happened?" Suzanne asked.

Emily shook her frazzled head. She'd been twisting the ends of her hair. "He was outside at the time, putting my bag in my trunk for me."

Suzanne frowned at her soda. "Did you tell him about it?"

"No." Emily grabbed her sweating glass from the coffee table and nearly spilled it. "I just said a quick good-bye, got in my car, and called you guys. I don't know what I would have done if you hadn't been around."

As Jane sipped her soda, it gave her an instant brain freeze. She'd hoped that the icy drinks would cool their heels and help them calm down, but it wasn't working very well.

Emily said, "I've been worried all along that Damien could be a demon, and now this happens right after I sleep with him." She openly fretted. "And it was the most amazing night of my life, too. God forgive me for saying this, but I'm afraid I won't be able to fight the temptation to be with him again. Me, the good Catholic girl who goes to church every Sunday. My poor grand-mother is probably rolling over in her grave."

"I understand how conflicted you are," Suzanne told her. "I know firsthand how it feels to get mixed up in their magic. But if one of them is harboring a dark entity, you can't be sure it's Damien."

"But it was his painting."

"Yes, but the groom is wearing a mask." The blonde shud-dered a little. "That could represent any of them."

"I'm still scared it's Damien. Do you think he made the groom move? And if he did, what was he trying to accomplish?

Why would he rouse my suspicion after he told me the demon was dead?"

"Maybe no one made it move," Suzanne said. "Maybe it just happened on its own, the way the song did with me."

Jane spoke. "Whatever is going on, these men are mired in it."

Emily clutched her glass. "Their names aren't even their names. Damien said that they changed them when they were younger because they needed to start over."

Now Jane understood why the Internet information she'd uncovered on Marcus was limited. He and his friends were living under aliases. Determined to do more than just sit and talk about it, she took a stand. "You know what I'm going to do tonight? I'm going to head over to Aeonian and see what kind of information I can dig up on them."

"What if Marcus is there?" Emily asked.

"I'll tell him what I'll be telling everyone else—that I'm doing research for the article. Besides, my deadline really is closing in. It's a perfect excuse to play reporter."

Jane entered the club, stepped farther into the lobby, and zeroed in on the blonde behind the counter. Picking her brain seemed like a good place to start. Asking her if Marcus was around wouldn't hurt, either.

"Hey," the girl greeted her.

"Hey yourself." Jane moved closer. The blonde was topless

except for a pair of burlesque-style pasties, tassels and all. Lord only knew what the bottom half of her ensemble entailed. The counter blocked the rest of her. "Have you seen Marcus?"

"No. Why? Were you supposed to meet up?"

Grateful for the Marcus reprieve, Jane shook her head. "Actually, the reason I stopped by was to interview people. I'm writing an article about Aeonian for *L.A. Underground*, and it would be great if I could get your input."

"Sure. But if anyone comes in while we're talking, I'll have to stop to greet them, or check to see if they have a guest pass if they're not a member." As she walked out from around the counter, the rest of her outfit came into view: butt-short hot pants, both cheeks exposed, and thigh-high boots. "I'm Candy, by the way. Sometimes people call me Eye Candy."

"I can see why." Even the stoic-faced bouncer on the other side of the room couldn't stop himself from sneaking a peek.

The blonde smiled, and Jane removed a pen and small notepad from her purse. They sat on a velvet settee, and the interview started with, "How long have you worked here?"

"About a year. Being a groupie is in my blood. My mom was a rock groupie. Totally gorgeous in her day. Big hair, big makeup, big fake tits." Candy cupped her own bodacious boobs. Apparently she'd inherited her mother's plastic surgeon. "Mom can't remember who she was with when I was conceived, so I don't know who my dad is. But he's a rocker for sure. She only did the stars. She didn't waste her time with roadies and management and shit."

Okay, then. Jane pretended to write something on her pad.

Bright eyed, Candy continued, "I'm just as picky. My favorite conquests are the supernaturals who are rumored to be real." She gave a sexy little shiver. "Being with them is a rush."

Jane leaned forward. Now the conversation was going somewhere. "Have any of the rumored superntaurals ever admitted that they're real?"

"No. But why would they? Aeonian is supposed to be their safe haven."

"According to who?"

"Everyone who believes the rumors."

"Do you believe them, Candy?"

"I don't know. Do you?"

Jane chose her denial carefully. "No, but it fascinates me."

"I can understand why. You're Marcus's new sub, and the mystery surrounding him and Jake and Damien will probably never be solved."

"Have you ever tried to solve it?"

"Sort of. I tried to have a foursome with them. I wanted to be with all of them at the same time to see if I could tell which one of them was the most demonic. But they didn't want to do it."

"Why not?"

"Because other groupies have tried the same thing, and the guys think it's an invasion of their brotherhood. If a groupie wants them, then she can be with each of them separately."

"Is that what you ended up doing?"

"Yes, but they're so different from each other, I didn't even try to compare them later." She went shivery again. "They all know how to make a girl come."

Indeed. Jane thought about the things she'd been allowing Marcus to do to her. But before she let those thoughts consume her, she straightened her spine and adjusted her notepad. "Do you know anything about their backgrounds?"

"No. But Noah would."

"Noah?"

"My boss. The man who owns the club. He screens all of the members."

"Is he here tonight?"

"He's here every night."

"Where can I find him?"

"He spends a lot of time in his office. That's on the fourth floor. His private quarters are up there, too. But by now he's probably in the Shifter Bar."

"And in which direction would that be?" Jane mentally prepared herself for the maze of hallways, stairwells, and rooms.

"It's through the disco and all the way to the left. The door has a mosaic on it made from fur, feathers, teeth, claws, bones, hooves, snakeskin—a bunch of different animal stuff."

"Sounds creepy."

Candy shrugged. "It's where the animal shapeshifters hang out when they're not off with a groupie somewhere. It's also where groupies go to meet those types of shifters."

"What does Noah look like?"

"It depends. Sometimes he's part mountain lion and some-times he just looks like himself."

"What's his appearance tonight?"

"He was himself earlier, but he might have changed." The blonde pursed her lips. "There are rumors that he's real, too."

Jane kept her features blank. "Describe him to me both ways."

"He's in his late twenties. Tall and dark skinned. He's Native American, but I don't know what tribe he's from. He doesn't talk about it. Anyway, he has long dark hair and exotic features, even when he's not a cat. So when he's in transformation, he's even wilder looking: slanted gold eyes, blondish streaks in his hair, sharp teeth, claws."

"Is he friendly?"

"I don't think he's ever bitten anyone or anything."

That wasn't what Jane meant, but she let the question slide. She would decide for herself how personable the club owner was.

"He has his pick of groupies," Candy said. "He's handsome and uber rich, too. But he doesn't play around with any of the girls who work here, so I've never been with him."

"Do you want to be with him?"

"I'd rather leave things as they are. It's nice to have a boss who isn't trying to get into your pants. That hardly ever happens to me. I've heard he's an amazing lover, though." Candy's sexy tremors returned. "They say that when he's in bed, he moves all rangy and mountain-lionish, and if you put your head on his chest, you can hear this deep rumble, like a big cat purring."

Jane didn't comment.

"It's weird, though," Candy said. "Because sometimes I think Noah is getting tired of women throwing themselves at him."

"Like he longs for more challenging prey? Maybe a regular girl instead of a groupie?"

"Exactly. Of course if he's real, I don't think that would work out very well. But don't tell him I said that, okay? I don't want to make him feel bad about wanting a regular girl."

"I won't say a word." Especially since Jane had thought of herself as regular girl before she'd gotten tangled up with Marcus. "I'm going to go look for Noah now."

"Okay." Candy jiggled back to her post, giving the bouncer another eyeful.

About five minutes later, Jane located the Shifter Bar and went inside. The room was dim and misty and packed with men, making her feel like a gazelle in a room full of cheetahs.

At a scarred wooden table, a trio of guys swathed in crocodile skin turned to look at her, and she had the urge to run. Crocodiles ate gazelles, too.

But in spite of the carnivorous energy, she maintained her outward cool and glanced around for Noah. Since Candy seemed uncertain if her boss would be a man or a beast tonight, she scanned the crowd for someone who fit either description.

Then she caught sight of an imposing figure seated at the bar.

She couldn't see his face because his back was to her, but she noticed that his long black hair was colored with tawny high-lights.

She approached him, but she wasn't able to get his attention. Occupying the barstool next to him was a man in a coyote mask who checked her out with the same hungry interest as the croco-diles.

"Did you know that coyotes are tricksters?" he asked.

She shook her head.

"Have you ever partied with one?"

Once again, she shook her head. But before his flirtation pro-gressed, she said, "I belong to someone already."

"And who might that be?"

"Marcus Monroe."

"Ah, yes, the master demon."

Jane frowned. That made Marcus sound like the king of a demon society. Not good, considering why she was here. She glanced deliberately at Noah. He'd yet to reveal his face or con-firm his identity, but she was certain it was him. She was also certain that he was tuned in to the conversation.

The coyote said, "Why aren't you in the dungeon?"

"Because Marcus isn't here tonight."

"He isn't going to like that his sub is prowling the Shifter Bar."

"I'm not prowling. I was looking for Noah."

The man in charge finally turned around, and his appearance nearly knocked Jane off her feet. He wore his transformation flawlessly well. It was impossible to tell where the special effects ended and his natural features began.

Were they special effects? Or was he real? She didn't know what to believe anymore. He was primitively handsome, and far too catlike.

With clawed fingers, he motioned for the coyote to give up his seat for Jane. The other man did as he was told, sniffing her hair as he passed.

Noah offered her the now-empty chair next to him. He asked her if she wanted a drink, and she went for the same lusty lime mocktail Marcus had gotten her the first time she was at Aeonian. Noah ordered scotch for himself, specifying a forty-year-old variety that she assumed was rare and expensive. But it was his club, and he could afford whatever he wanted.

The bartender reacted lickety-split.

Jane accepted her drink, but before Noah reached for his, he retracted his claws, giving her a start.

Regardless, she did her best to seem unaffected. "That's quite a trick."

"I'm not the trickster. Coyote is."

She changed the subject and introduced herself.

After she recited her name, he replied, "I know who you are."

"Do you know about the article I'm writing, too?"

"Marcus told me about it before he applied for your membership and before I screened you."

"Then you wouldn't mind if I asked you a few questions?"

"About the club? No, but that's not why you sought me out. You're interested in discussing Marcus and his friends." He was either highly perceptive or Candy had called him and given him a heads-up. Jane pegged him for perceptive.

She said, "Since you screen your members, I was hoping you'd be willing to share some tidbits about them."

A hint of fang showed when he talked. "You mean if one of them is a genuine demon?"

She tried to sound casual. "I don't believe any of that, but I have to admit the rumors would add a bit of spice to my article. You can't blame me for wondering what sorts of things turned up in their backgrounds."

He finished his scotch. "I'm not at liberty to discuss them or anyone else with you. I protect my members' privacies."

Irked that he wouldn't budge, she challenged him. "Are you protecting your members' privacies or are you just protecting your own kind?"

"Demons are not my kind." His cat-shaped eyes mocked hers. "As you can see, I'm portraying a completely different kind of being. Now go home, Jane, and come back when your master is with you."

She was more than ready to go home, and angry at herself for letting her frustration show, especially in front of the owner of the club.

Twelve

Jane stood at her front door, digging through her purse for her house key.

Annoyed that she couldn't find it, she gave her purse a hard rattle, tempted to dump the entire contents onto the stoop. She was so frazzled she could scream. This day had gone from bad to worse to absolutely terrible.

A deep male voice loomed out of the dark. "Relax, Jane. Your key is probably wedged in the fold of your wallet."

Her breath rushed out.

She spun around and glared at Marcus, her pulse jumping all over the place. "You nearly gave me a heart attack." His specialty, apparently. "How long have you been there?"

"Not long. You were too preoccupied to hear me when I walked up."

It almost seemed as if he'd appeared out of thin air. Then again, maybe he did. She was too confused to know what was going on anymore.

Ignoring him, she searched for her key again and found it wedged in her wallet. She glanced suspiciously at him.

"Lucky guess," he said.

"What are you doing here?"

"Noah called me and said you were at the club. He said you were asking questions about Jake, Damien, and me."

She looked him up and down. He was dressed in his usual attire, making the tall, dark presentation he always made. "I was doing research for my article."

"That's not how it seemed to Noah."

"So maybe I was just trying to learn more about you."

"Why? Are you having doubts about me and my friends? Do you think we're lying about what happened when we were kids?"

Since she couldn't betray Emily and mention the painting, she referred to other sources. "Songs jumping off pages and teenagers conjuring and killing a demon isn't within my usual realm of thinking."

"Then quit thinking about it and come home with me."

She remained on alert. "To do what?"

"We could curl up on the couch and watch a movie. Maybe

microwave a bag of kettle corn. Sweet-and-salty snacks are my favorite."

Hers, too, but she wasn't going to give him the satisfaction of knowing it. Instead, she protected herself from a side of him she'd never seen. "What kind of movie? A slasher film?"

He rolled his eyes, and she wondered about the damage that had been supposedly done to them.

He said, "I was thinking more along the lines of a comedy."

"Seriously?"

"I like goofy movies."

"Me, too."

"Then let's hang out and watch one."

She gave in and accepted the invitation, curious about the environment in which he lived. "I'll come over, but I'm not staying the night. I want this to be a nonsexual date."

"It will be," he assured her.

He waited while she changed out of her club gear and slipped on a casual outfit.

They hit the road, and she followed him to his residence, a charming old house in a tree-lined neighborhood.

Once they were inside, she glanced around his living room. The entertainment center was the focal point, along with a gray sofa and matching recliner.

"We can stream a movie on Netflix," he said. "Or you can look through my DVDs to see if there's anything that appeals to you. I don't mind watching something I've seen before."

Curious to view his collection, she walked over to the entertainment center and discovered his DVDs were arranged by genre, and within each genre, they were alphabetized.

Could he be any more organized? Of course she already knew how meticulous he was about his clothes. It would stand to reason that he was that way about everything.

She scanned the comedies and removed *The Hangover*. "I absolutely love this movie."

He smiled. "Me, too."

They agreed to watch it, but first they headed to the kitchen, which had tiled floors and an oak table. He offered her a soda and poured it into a glass with ice.

Jane took a sip and wandered over to a sliding glass door that showcased a small deck. "Do you barbecue?"

"Sometimes."

She noticed a solid white door in the corner of the room and made her way over there. "Where does this go?"

"To the basement."

"Wow. A basement in L.A. That's a rarity."

He removed a box of kettle corn from the cabinet. "The people I bought the house from used it as a fallout shelter."

"What do you use it for?"

He tilted his head, and she realized what a stupid question it was. Obviously he had a dungeon.

"Silly me," she said.

"It's okay."

Since he didn't offer any information, she got curious. "What sort of equipment do you have?"

"The main piece is a custom-made bondage bed with attachments and accessories."

"Really?" She was still standing relatively close to the door. "Can I see it?"

"I thought you wanted to keep things light."

Her dander went up. "I'm more than capable of looking at a bondage bed without wanting to use it."

He set the kettle corn aside. "Don't get testy. I was just asking."

Before they descended the stairs, he flipped a light switch and illuminated their way. They reached the bottom, and there, amid bright red walls, was a king-sized bed with steel posts. Mirrored panels served as a headboard and created a canopy. Beneath the platform-height frame was a metal cage.

"What do you think?" he asked.

What she thought was how stupid she was for insisting on coming down here. She actually envisioned being locked under the bed.

Refusing to give herself away, especially after the fuss she'd made, she feigned a causal response. "It's an interesting design."

"A suspension sling fits up there." He pointed to the top rails. "It was fun working out the details with the company that built it. The mirrors are safety glass, so rough play isn't a problem."

Rough play was exactly what she was craving, but she wasn't about to admit it. "What type of bed do you have in your room?"

"A regular one. It wouldn't make sense sleeping in a bondage bed when I'm by myself." He indicated a trunk in the corner. "That's where I keep my toys."

Items that weren't supposed to matter tonight. "Since you have all of this, why do you use the private rooms at Aeonian?"

"I like the club atmosphere. Besides, I only bring special subs here." He turned to face her. "None of them have been as special as you are. But I already told you that we were fated."

Being referred to as his favorite sub intensified her secret hunger to be locked up, but his repeated destiny claim baffled her. "Do you still think the other couples are fated, too?"

"Yes, but it's up to them to see it for themselves."

A soundless moment passed between them. Then he asked, "Should we go upstairs and watch the movie now?"

She nodded, as confused as ever.

Emily had given into temptation, just as she'd feared she would. She was back at Damien's house and praying for her own salvation.

She parked her car and took hesitant steps. Struggling to keep her emotional balance, she rang the bell.

He opened the door. With his wavy chestnut hair and holey jeans, he was a captivating sight.

"Hi." He greeted her with a smile. "Are you ready?"

Was she? She crossed the threshold, and he took her hand

and led her down the hall. Since they bypassed the living room, she was able to avoid the painting. She didn't want the groom looking at her again.

Soon, they were stripped to the bone and climbing into the bathtub.

While he knelt between her legs, she stood as motionless as she could. He was shaving her pubic region.

He wanted to do some body painting on her, and he claimed that she needed to be smooth for the design.

As he swiped the razor across her mound, she glanced down at him and noticed how focused he was on his task.

When it came time for him to do the inside of her labia, he rolled the lips open and lathered the area. Ever so gently, he moved the razor along her flesh, taking the tiny hairs off.

After she was completely smooth, he turned on the water and used a handheld sprayer to rinse her off.

They got out of the tub and patted dry. He removed an astringent from the cabinet and dabbed it onto her with a cotton ball, soothing the areas he'd shaved.

Still naked, they went into his studio, and he gathered his art supplies.

As he positioned himself in between her legs once again, only this time with a paintbrush, he said, "For now, this is the only part of you I'm going paint. It shouldn't take long."

She recalled a conversation they'd had about him painting

her entire body, creating art that would take hours. She assumed this was his way of helping her get used to modeling for him. But did he have to choose the most intimate part of her?

Of course he did. He was an erotic artist, consumed with lust, and her vagina was his canvas.

He dipped into the paint, and her skin tingled from the featherlight bristles on his brush, but it was his proximity that affected her the most. He was so close, his breathing fluttered across her skin.

He worked diligently, mixing paint and using precise strokes, and soon a beautiful pink flower began to appear.

When it was complete, he stood up, leaned over and kissed her romantically on the mouth. She sighed against his lips, falling deeper into temptation.

He led her to his bedroom, where he instructed her to sit in front of the closet door mirror. He sat down, too, and scooted in behind her, slipping his arms around her waist.

"Open your legs," he said.

She did as she was told, then gazed at the flower he'd created. Now that she could see it up close, she noticed how truly detailed it was. The outside petals were various shades of pink but as it neared her labia, the pigment blended into her skin, making her flesh look like the center of the flower.

"It's an orchid," he said. "They're symbols of perfection."

She leaned back against him. He made her feel perfect.

Damien. A man who might have a demon inside him. She turned her head, and they kissed, even more romantically than before.

God help her for letting this happen.

He ended the kiss and met her gaze in the mirror.

"Look how right we are together," he said.

No, she thought. It was wrong. So terribly wrong. Little by little, he was stealing his way into her heart.

He nuzzled her cheek, pressing the side of his face against hers. "You have such soft skin. And luxurious hair." He examined the color. "It's like espresso with chocolate."

"My grandma used to make a cake with those ingredients." The woman who'd taught her to fear demons. Yet here Emily was, in the arms of danger.

"Do you have the recipe?"

"Not written down, but I know how to make it. It's a dark chocolate cake, but it has the most delicious fluffy white frosting."

"Then we'll make it sometime. We'll cut it into big, thick pieces, then put it on pretty glass plates and feed it to each other."

Like a bride and groom on their wedding day?

The thought panicked her, but then he reached around to stroke her, and she fell victim to his charm. Instinctively, she rolled her hips toward his hand.

He rubbed the center of the orchid, making it bloom, making her dizzy with desire, but that was what he did best.

She watched in the mirror. She saw everything: the way he

circled her clit, the way her body flushed with arousal, the way her heart kept coming unglued.

He rubbed harder and deeper, and she climaxed so powerfully, she gasped at her own reflection.

Before the shock waves subsided, he lifted her to her feet and led her to bed, where the madness continued. They climbed under the covers and kissed. The taste of him filled her like fire. She opened her legs, offering him the orchid, and he used a lubricated condom, making his penetration warm and slick.

They made love in different positions, with him bending her body to suit both of their needs.

On and on it went, spiraling out of control.

Afterward, she fell asleep in his arms, and when she awakened hours later, he was gazing at her through those strange black eyes.

She waited for him to say something, but he remained quiet.

She took it upon herself to ask, "Why are you looking at me like that?"

"Because you're pretty, and you're making me crave something sweet." He kept gazing at her. "Let's go into the kitchen and get a snack."

She glanced at the clock. "It's the middle of the night."

"Come on, Emily, have some cookies and milk with me."

She conceded, and they got out of bed. She slipped on the kimono robe she'd borrowed from him last time, and he put on his tattered jeans, which added to his already tousled appeal.

Once they were in the kitchen, he rummaged through the cabinets. But he didn't produce any cookies.

"I have an idea," he said. "We can make the chocolate espresso cake."

Because of the wedding visual it produced, she tried to steer him in another direction. "That's not a quick snack. It takes a while to make, and you might not even have all of the ingredients."

"I'll bet I do."

Sure enough, he was right. And there was no talking him out of it. He wanted what he wanted.

They gathered everything and got started. She combined flour, baking soda, and salt in a bowl and set it aside, then he melted the chocolate while she beat butter, sugar, and brown sugar with an electric mixer. Eggs, sour cream, vanilla, and a freshly brewed cup of espresso completed the batter.

He tasted it with his finger and smiled. "This is going to be amazing."

She made a foolish joke in her mind and wondered if they should be making devil's food cake instead. With his boyish dimple and disheveled hair, he looked positively wicked.

For the umpteenth time that night, she told herself how wrong it was to be with him. Yet she stayed by his side.

After both pans went into the oven, they prepared the white buttercream frosting. Later, after the cake cooled, they filled the layers and iced the top and the sides. Artist that he was, he used simple kitchen tools to create fancy swirls and an intricate lattice design, making a masterpiece.

Staying true to his word, he cut two large slices and placed them on etched glass plates. The presentation was beyond beautiful.

"Why don't we have wine in lieu of milk?" he said, and removed the cork from a Cabernet Sauvignon. "This vintage is perfect with chocolate."

Damien placed everything on the dining room table, and they sat next to each other. He poured the wine into the chalices he obviously favored, and she watched him, knowing what came next.

He lifted his fork and offered her a frothy bite of the cake. Feeling like his forbidden bride, she ate it, and as the flavor melted in her mouth, she moaned her decadent pleasure.

It was so good, it was to die for.

Thirteen

Jane sat at a table in the coffee bar she frequented, drinking a latte and frowning at her laptop. Although she had multiple projects in the works, all of them with deadlines looming, it was tough to concentrate on anything except the Aeonian article.

Or more accurately, it was tough to concentrate on anything except Marcus. Ever since meeting him, her common sense had pole-vaulted out the window. First she'd been fixated on him snapping a whip across her butt, something he'd yet to do, and now she was fantasizing about being locked in a cage.

And while she was having those fantasies, she was caught in the vortex of the demon situation. She scowled at the keyboard again. Talk about being distracted.

A moment later, she felt someone approach her. She hoped it wasn't Marcus. All she needed was him appearing out of nowhere.

She glanced up. An unfamiliar man stood there. He looked like a young professional, the clean-cut type in a button-down shirt and khaki slacks. But pesky people came in all shapes and sizes.

"I'm sorry to disturb you," he said, "but there's something I'd like to discuss with you."

"Yes?"

"It's about your master and his friends."

If she'd been clutching her coffee, she would have dropped it. Her hands had gone shaky. "Who are you?"

"Stanley Truxton." He leaned into her table. "Also known as Coyote."

The weirdo from the Shifter Bar? She narrowed her eyes at him. "How did you know where to find me?"

"I asked around at the club about you, then I Googled your name. I came across your blog and you mentioned that you sometimes come here to work. I took a chance that you'd be here today."

She chastised herself for making something like that public. But in her defense, it was an old post, long before she'd ever even heard of Aeonian or become Marcus's sub.

"May I join you?" he asked.

Although she was curious about what he had to say, she was

still leery of him. She resorted to, "Fine, but that doesn't mean I trust you."

He pulled up a chair and sat across from her. "I didn't know that you belonged to Marcus when I first saw you. I wouldn't have hit on you if I did."

"You sniffed my hair."

"I'm supposed to be part coyote and that's what a coyote would do. I was just staying in character." He lowered his voice. "Did you know that Aeonian is chock-full of real supernaturals, and that one of the men you and your friends are messing around with is a real demon?"

She refused to bat an eye, even if she was twitching inside. "I'm well aware of the rumors."

"And I heard about the article you're writing."

"From Noah?"

"From Candy. She said you interviewed her."

"I interviewed Noah, too."

"He's one of them." He folded his hands on the tabletop. "I have proof of who the supernaturals are."

Although she was still openly distrustful of him, her heart skipped a slew of beats, and she waited for him to explain.

He said, "When I was a child, a witchcraft goddess cast a spell on me, and now I can sense anyone who transcends the laws of nature."

She didn't know what to say, so she kept quiet.

He continued, "I applied for a membership at the club because

I heard about the rumors and I wanted to see for myself. But I didn't want to be a groupie, so I became a coyote. A trickster, as it were. I'm the only mortal at the club who has the power to tell who is immortal and who isn't."

She asked the burning question. "So who's the real demon?"

He made a face. "I don't know."

"You just said that you could tell."

"Normally I can. But the bond between Marcus, Jake, and Damien is too tight. Although I can feel the demonic energy that surrounds them, they protect each other so well I can't localize it. I don't think anyone could, not even another demon."

"Are there other demons at Aeonian?" she asked, just to see what he would say.

He shook his head. "But there are plenty of other creatures to be wary of. The largest population is vampires."

"Tell me what else you know about Marcus and his friends."

"Aside from their energy and their sexual reputations? Nothing." He scooted his chair in a bit more, and it made a slight squeal against the floor. "I'm sure Noah knows who the demon is, but only because they told him. He wouldn't have allowed them into the club without verifying their history. Of course he would never betray their secret."

She'd gotten the same impression about Noah. "Why did you want to discuss this with me?"

"I figured you'd be interested."

"Have you told anyone else at the club?"

"That I have the ability to detect supernatural energy? I've mentioned it to some of the groupies, but it hasn't made much of a difference. They either believe the rumors or they don't. The immortals don't care what I say, either, because they would never admit the truth." He watched her, clearly gauging her reaction. "What do you think?"

She wasn't about to tell him that he'd just jumbled her already confused mind. "What I think is that I need to get back to work."

"Then I'll leave you be." He stood up and gave her a slight bow as he said good-bye.

After he exited the coffeehouse, she grabbed her cell phone, eager to arrange a meeting with Suzanne and Emily.

Later that evening, the women gathered at their favorite Mexican restaurant during happy hour, sipping margaritas and waiting for their entrees to arrive. As usual, Jane was the designated driver and her drink was minus the tequila.

After she recited what Coyote had told her, she couldn't deny her concern. "A 'trickster' isn't the best of source of information, but what he said sounds plausible, like their energy being connected, and the likelihood that Noah knows which man is the demon." She turned to Emily. "I think you've been right from the beginning. I think the demon rumor is real."

"Me, too," Suzanne said, adding her validation. "There are just too many things leading us in that direction."

Emily replied, "As fearful as I am that Damien is the one, I keep hoping and praying that he isn't. I don't know what I'll do if we find out for sure that it's him. I'm already struggling with how this is affecting my faith. I feel like such a hypocrite."

Suzanne's mind was obviously on Jake. "Do you think it's true that they were tortured and that Jake suffered the most? Or do you think Damien made that up?"

Jane replied, "It's tough to know how much of what was said is true, including Marcus's destiny claims. He seems to be implying that it involves more than sex."

Emily placed a jittery hand against her heart. "On our first night together Damien talked about never letting me go."

"That makes me wonder if Jake is the demon," Suzanne said. "He's so detached compared to the other two. And if the torture stuff is true then that could've been when the demon's spirit entered him. It could also be why 'pain' was the last word that appeared in his song before all of the lyrics spun off the page. Then again . . ." She looked at Jane. "Maybe it's Marcus. He seems like the leader, and he's the most commanding of the three. Plus he's capable of hypnotic suggestions."

Jane couldn't argue with Suzanne's assessment. Any of them could be hosting the entity, and if their energy really was as connected as Coyote had claimed, then how were she and her friends ever going to figure it out?

Soon their meals arrived, and after the waiter left, they ate in silence. Jane didn't bother commenting on how good her enchilada was; what was the point of making small talk? Their thoughts were elsewhere.

Finally she shattered the quiet and asked Suzanne, "When are you going to see Jake again?"

"Tomorrow night. We're going to the club." The question was returned. "When are you going to see Marcus again?"

"I don't know. We haven't made any plans. But if I was smart, I'd end it with him." Then she could quit fantasizing about riding crops and metal cages, and she could quit caring about who or what Marcus was.

A second later, she got a brainstorm. "Maybe I can call Marcus's bluff about the destiny issue. If he honestly believes that all of us are fated, then I can threaten to stop seeing him and see how he reacts. And you two can do the same thing with Damien and Jake. We can take a position of power."

"That won't work with Jake," Suzanne said. "He's not as vested in me as your guys are with you."

"It's better than doing nothing. Besides, if he isn't ready to end your affair, it still might affect him."

Emily moved her rice around on her plate. "I'm probably dooming myself, but I think it's too soon for us to make threats."

Clearly, neither she nor Suzanne was ready to take the chance of losing their men, demon or not. Crazy as it was, Jane wasn't ready to throw in the towel, either.

She backpedaled. "I'm not saying that we have to do this right away. We'll keep it in the back of our minds, and when the timing seems right, we'll give it a go."

The other two agreed, and an unsteady plan was hatched.

Suzanne entered the club with Jake, determined to forget about the conversation she'd had with Jane and Emily, at least for tonight. All that mattered this evening was enjoying the illicitness of being with Jake.

They took the stairs to the second floor, where voyeur activity reigned supreme.

As they reached the landing, she thought about the last time they were here and how exciting it was to watch the fairy and her groupie lover. "What type of play should we watch tonight?" she asked. "Group, threesomes, or couples?"

"I was thinking that we could be the couple being watched. I already reserved one of the bedrooms in case you're interested."

Suzanne nearly swayed on her high heels. "Why didn't you mention this earlier?"

"I thought spur of the moment would be easier for you. So, do you want to do it?"

Take off her clothes and mess around in front of a one-way mirror? That was a bit more illicit that she'd imagined. "What time is our reservation?"

He glanced at his watch. "In about an hour. Plenty of time for a drink if you need one."

Or two or three, she thought. "Let me think about it while I'm getting intoxicated. Is there a bar on this floor?"

"There's a bar on every floor."

He guided her in the direction of the alcohol, and her heart bumped against her chest. The idea of putting on a show for other people was both sexy and scary.

The bar was softly lit and retro chic. It was crowded, but luckily they found an empty table near the back.

As Suzanne set down her purse, Jake asked, "Is the lipstick I gave you in there?"

The pink jelly vibrator. "Yes. But you're not going to ask me to use it right now, are you?"

"No. But you can use it when we're in the private room if you want."

The sexy, scary feeling came back. "I just want a drink."

"No problem." He signaled for their waitress.

Suzanne ordered a Long Island iced tea because it had a bunch of different kinds of liquor in it, and Jake got his usual beer.

Luckily, it didn't take long for their drinks to arrive. Jake paid the tab, and the waitress disappeared.

"I wonder who's going to watch us," he said.

Instead of reminding him that she hadn't agreed to be watched, Suzanne swigged her cocktail and glanced around the bar.

At a nearby table, two male groupies and a woman in a skillfully tattered vampire costume were exchanging rough kisses. If she was able to choose the voyeurs, would she pick a feral trio like them?

Curious to see if anyone else grabbed her attention, she scanned the crowd and noticed a man dressed like a prince. He wasn't with anyone, but a groupie with flowing blonde hair kept stealing amorous glances at him. Normally a prince wouldn't be considered a supernatural being, but with his gilded clothes and powerful stance, he had a dragon-slaying aura. It made Suzanne wonder, for a split second, if he was real.

She turned her attention back to Jake, and he smiled.

"You're going to do it," he said.

Because he'd already planted the seed? Because she was already starting to fantasize about it? He'd called her easy when she'd first met him. Easy prey. Easy to seduce.

She wanted to fight it, but when he turned to kiss her, she lost her sense of reason. As always, he made her feel hot and erotic. As his tongue swept her mouth, she placed her hand on his knee. He reciprocated, sliding his hand along her thigh.

Were the vampire and her companions still kissing? Or had they stopped to watch her and Jake? And what about the magic prince and the blonde?

Suddenly Suzanne didn't care who the voyeurs were, as long as she was being intimate with Jake.

"You're right," she whispered. "I'm going to do it."

"Without getting drunk?"

She nodded and pushed her drink aside. Being intoxicated defeated the purpose.

The hour passed quickly, and soon Jake was unlocking the door to their room and escorting her inside.

It wasn't the same room the fairy and her groupie lover had used, but it was similar, with a luxuriously draped bed, Gothic accents, and a fully mirrored wall.

Suzanne knew a viewing room was on the other side of it. "Do you think our voyeurs are already in there?"

"Probably."

Which meant they were already being watched. Her stomach flipped, making her feel like an actress with a tumbling dose of stage fright. "Maybe I should have gotten drunk."

"Just relax and try not to think about it."

"But I don't know what to do now that we're here."

He stood behind her. "You could strip down to your bra and panties."

"In front of the mirror?"

"Yes."

Her stomached flipped again, but she followed his suggestion and shimmied out of her dress, which left her in a zebra-print bra, matching panties, and thigh-high hose.

Still standing behind her, Jake slipped his arms around her waist. "You look like an underwear model."

She leaned back against him. She worked hard on keeping her figure. "Thank you."

He kissed the side of her neck. "You smell delicious, too. I like your perfume. What is it?"

"Gucci Guilty." She thought about the ad campaign associated with the fragrance. "It's supposed to encourage a woman to experience the thrill of the forbidden."

He brought her body even closer to his. "Then it's working, isn't it?"

She gazed at their reflections and nodded. She hoped that whoever was watching was getting aroused by the way Jake was holding her.

"When are you going to get undressed?" she asked.

"After you use the vibrator."

He released her so she could remove it from her purse. She decided to behave as if it was actually lipstick. After she got it, she returned to the mirror, opened the tube and held it up to her mouth as if she was going to apply it to her lips. But then she switched directions and moved it down her body, sliding it into her panties.

She imagined that the voyeurs were leaning forward now. Jake was certainly paying attention. He had a noticeable hard-on.

With the flick of a switch, she turned on the device and held it against her clit, giving herself a sweet, soft massage.

Jake came up behind her again. She met his gaze in the mirror, and he pressed his distended fly against her rear, multiplying the pleasure.

While the toy gently hummed, he reached into her bra and

caressed her breasts. Her nipples went hard, and her knees went wonderfully weak.

"Do you like thinking about how much this is turning someone else on?" he asked.

Her skin tingled. "Yes." But most of all, she liked being with Jake.

He unhooked her bra, and the material slacked, giving him easier access to her breasts. She moaned and moved the vibrator in little circles.

"After you come, we're going to use that big fancy bed," he said. "We're going to climb all over each other."

Wild images twirled in her mind. "Can we sixty-nine?"

"Yes, ma'am," he responded in that southern way of his.

It didn't take long for Suzanne to climax. All she had to do was hold the vibrator in place and let Jake's voice wash over her. His hands, too. He continued to caress her.

As soon as she let herself go, maple-sweet spasms exploded at her core, blurring everything except a faint outline of their reflections.

Before she melted to the ground, Jake lifted her up and carried her to bed, and she thought about the magic prince in the bar. Was Jake her prince?

Her dark prince, she thought, as she looked into his eyes.

She put her head on his shoulder and struggled to clear her mind. He placed her on the bed, and she sank into the covers.

He undressed her completely. Dazed, she realized that she was still clutching the vibrator.

He took it from her and set it aside. Quickly, he shed his clothes and kissed her. Overwhelmed with every ripple of muscle, with every flesh-and-blood nuance that made him male, she pulled him closer.

They rolled over the bed, and he put his face between her legs. While he feasted on her, he maneuvered both of them into the position she craved.

She gripped the base of his penis and played with the head before she took him fully into her mouth. This was the first blow job she'd given him and she went mad with the feeling, especially with him sucking softly on her clit.

Once again, he'd managed to corrupt her, only this time the debasement went deeper. Suzanne was losing herself to a mysterious man and struggling with her attachment to him.

While strangers were watching.

Fourteen

Jane parked in front of Marcus's house. He hadn't invited her over, and she hadn't called ahead. This was an unannounced visit, and like the anxious woman she'd become, she'd packed an overnight bag and stuffed it in her trunk.

It wasn't as if she didn't have a right to stay with him. But she was appalled at herself for wanting to see him so badly.

The cage in his dungeon was driving her crazy.

It was bad enough that he might be a frigging demon, but did she have to obsess about being imprisoned by him, too?

Maybe this wasn't her fault. Maybe he really had been hypnotizing her this whole time. Maybe he'd even planted the suggestion of her coming over tonight.

Keeping the blame on him, she got out of the car and walked up to his front door. She rang the bell and waited.

When he answered, she was surprised by his appearance. Although his hair was banded into its usual ponytail and his contacts lenses were in place, he was casually attired. No black garb or heavy black boots.

If he'd been expecting her, wouldn't he be more prepared? Wouldn't he have made a more dom-like presentation?

"Hey," he said. "What's going on?"

She wasn't about to respond with something silly, like she just happened to be in the neighborhood, so she said, "I was in the mood to see you."

He invited her into the house, but he didn't react in a sexual way, and she wondered how she was supposed to manipulate the situation to suit her needs.

"Would you like a soda?" he asked. "Or some juice?"

"Juice sounds good." Simply to get near the kitchen where the dungeon door was.

She followed him to the fridge, and he opened it.

"Is pineapple okay?"

She nodded, and he poured her a glass. He got one for himself, too. But before he could steer her back to the living room, she walked over to the dining table and sat down. It was just a hop, skip, and a jump from where she wanted to be.

He sat across from her. "I know why you're here."

"You do?"

"Yes, and I don't want to play tonight."

Damn him. "Why not?"

"I just don't."

"You can show up at my house in the middle of the night and force me to my knees, but I can't get a little action when I need it?" She stood up. "Screw you, Marcus."

"Tonight is the anniversary of my parents' murders."

Stunned, she sat back down. "I'm so sorry." He'd barely talked about himself, and now he was ripping the bandage off of a gnashing wound. The memory in his voice was painfully evident.

"It was a carjacking." He released a laden breath and his chest rose and fell with the effort. "Dad was taking Mom out for a celebratory dinner. She was a newly licensed real estate agent, and she'd just sold her first house."

Her heart went out to him. "How old were you when it happened?"

"Fifteen. They were the most amazing people. Kind, loving, affectionate. They were all I had." He cleared his throat, then drank some juice.

She suspected that his mouth had gone dry. Hers certainly had.

He continued, "There wasn't anyone to take me in, so I became a ward of the state. I hated every single foster home I was in. That's why I ran away, and that's how I met Jake and Damien. They're my family now. I love them like brothers."

She thought about how deeply the men were protecting each other. "And they love you in the same way."

"We would die for each other if it came down to that."

Fear crawled up her spine, twisting around her vertebrae like a dark red vine. "Is it going to come down to that?"

He didn't respond, increasing her fear.

"Are you trying to scare me?" she asked.

In an unexpected show of affection, he reached across the table for her hand. "I was just making a point."

Their fingertips brushed. "So no one is going to die?"

"Everyone dies someday."

"Immortals don't."

"Some do."

"How do demons die?"

"It depends on how powerful they are." He locked his fingers with hers, creating a stronger connection. "But I don't want to talk about death anymore. I've seen enough of it to last a lifetime."

No one close to Jane had ever died. She didn't know that kind of pain, and she didn't want to know it. She came from a big family, and all of them were still in Cincinnati, where she was born.

She gazed quietly at her lover. He'd told her more about himself than she'd expected to hear, and that made her feel closer to him.

Far closer than she should.

He asked her to stay with him, and she readily agreed. He wanted to turn in early, and she understood why. It was obvious he was beat. She was, too. Emotionally, she was spent. This night had turned out far different than she'd planned.

She went out to the car to retrieve her bag, and a short time later, they were nestled in bed. His room was as organized as the rest of the house, and it was completely devoid of anything related to BDSM.

He turned out the light and reached for her, and she put her head in the crook of his arm. She closed her eyes. She'd forgotten all about the cage. But in the morning, her interest in it was renewed.

At first light, Marcus woke her up and led her straight to his basement.

Down the stairs they went, with Jane's nightshirt grazing her knees and her hair mussed from sleep. Marcus, on the other hand, was as sharp as a paper cut. While she'd been crashed out, he'd showered, shaved, and donned his signature black clothes and intimidating black boots. He looked every bit the master.

Once they were in the dungeon, he said, "I haven't decided what I should do to you."

Submissive excitement swirled through her blood. If he knew why she'd showed up last night, then he must be aware of her cage craving.

While her anticipation mounted, he went over to the trunk

that contained his toys. He crouched down and opened the lid. From where she stood, she couldn't see what types of items were inside, but she could tell that he was examining the contents with a critical eye. She didn't doubt that each toy was carefully wrapped and properly stored. Marcus wouldn't throw them haphazardly in a trunk.

He held up an anatomically designed dildo. "What do you think of this?"

"It's impressive." About the same length and girth as his cock, with a bulging head, veined texture, and hefty balls. "But I'd prefer to have you inside me."

"This is battery operated. It rotates and vibrates."

"But your body feels warm next to mine, and you haven't been inside me yet." Of all the things he'd done to her, intercourse wasn't one of them.

"You make getting fucked by your dom sound romantic."

She clarified her statement. "That isn't how I meant it." She tugged on her nightshirt. Suddenly she was nervous. "I kept the origami heart you gave me, though."

"Damien taught me how to make those. I can make all sorts of things." He put the dildo away and closed the trunk. "Even paper penises that slide up and down."

"Maybe next time you can give me one of those."

"Maybe I will." He stood up. "But we're getting off track."

She gazed at his empty hands. "You didn't get a toy."

"I'm going to lock you up first. Then you can't misbehave or distract me." Without further instruction, he came toward her and motioned to the cage.

Much too eager, she got down on the floor, opened the metal door, and crawled into the space. Although it was shallow and she had to stay on her knees or lie down, it was actually wide enough for two people. Two subs, she thought, with a territorial frown.

He bent down and closed the door. He put a padlock on it, too. After he resumed his stance, she peered out from the bars and gazed at his booted feet.

He disappeared from sight, and she heard him moving about the dungeon. Then everything went quiet. Was he back at the trunk?

Yes, he was. The hinges squealed as he opened the lid. She listened for evidence of what he'd picked, but it was impossible to tell. Soon he was striding up and down the length of the cage.

"I chose three toys," he said, as if he'd read her curious mind. He lowered a sleek black whip and ran it along the bars, revealing the first item.

Goose bumps scattered along her skin. Her fantasy had taken on a life of its own. He was like a lion tamer in the throes of his job.

"I could leave you in there all day," he said. "I could tease you for hours."

No, he couldn't, not if she used one of the safe words. But they both knew that she wasn't going to stop him.

Insanely aroused, she gazed at the whip as it passed.

"Take off your clothes, Jane."

Although it was difficult to undress in a prone position, she did as she was told, peeling off her panties and tugging her nightshirt over her head.

"Now close your eyes and no matter what happens, don't open them."

She obeyed his command, and while she lay there in the dark, he continued to walk the length of the cage, the sound of his footsteps intensifying.

Then he stopped.

And cracked the whip on the ground.

She flinched something fierce, but she kept her eyes squeezed tight. In the next bout of silence, she counted the beats of her heart.

He didn't crack the whip again. But he clanked something against the bars, creating a steel-against-steel noise.

The second toy?

A few moments later, she heard him unlocking the cage and swinging open the door.

"Don't move," he said.

Jane went motionless. She sensed him crawling toward her, and she yearned for his nearness.

He straddled her, then snapped circular objects around her wrists and locked her to the sides of the cage.

Handcuffs.

A silky blindfold came next, signaling the third toy and shutting out the light behind her still-closed eyes. Everything went pitch-black.

His body was heavy against hers, and his clothes scratched her nakedness, but he was the perfect master. His mouth sought hers, and he kissed her. Jane was glad the cage was big enough for two people.

"Do you still want me inside you?" he asked.

"Yes."

"It's not going to be romantic."

"I already told you that I don't care about that."

In the next instant, Jane became aware of the motion of his hand on his fly and his pants being pushed down. She heard the tearing of the condom packet, too.

He nudged her legs open, slid between them, and entered her hard and deep. She lifted her hips to greet his penetration. As he moved, the handcuffs scraped against her wrists. They weren't padded and neither was the floor. She clenched her bare ass with every thrust.

She was getting fucked by her dom, and it spite of how non-romantic it was supposed to be, it was the most beautiful sex she'd ever had.

Alone in her apartment, Emily considered everything that was going on. Jane and Suzanne had told her about their recent encounters with Marcus and Jake. The most surprising information was the details about Marcus's family. Of course Emily felt for him because she'd lost her parents, too.

But at the moment, her biggest concern was Damien. She'd called him earlier and invited him to come over, and now she was waiting for him to arrive. But she'd already warned him that this wasn't about sex. She'd asked him to attend a local craft fair with her. She wasn't sure what she was trying to accomplish, other than a neurotic attempt to manufacture a seemingly normal date.

Fussing over her appearance, she checked her reflection in the bathroom mirror. She looked like her wholesome self. Considering Damien's attraction to her innocence, she didn't know if that was good or bad.

The doorbell rang and she dashed off to answer it, her stomach twisting into a nervous knot.

She flung open the door, and her gaze locked with Damien's for what seemed like an exaggerated amount of time. After he entered the living room, he kissed her softly on the lips. If there was a demon inside him, it was masking itself far too well.

They separated, and before she had the chance to show him around, he wandered over to the electric fireplace, a freestanding unit she'd purchased to make her apartment seem homier.

She followed him, and he focused on the mantel, which held a collection of photographs.

"Is this you?" he asked.

She nodded. "That's my first-grade picture. I'd just started losing my baby teeth."

He didn't comment, but he seemed fascinated by her gap-toothed smile. The next framed image was taken about a year later.

He studied it with an intense expression. "You look like a miniature bride here."

The observation made her uncomfortable coming from him. She wished she'd had the foresight to hide the picture before he'd shown up. "It was my First Holy Communion. White dresses are a symbol of purity, and the veil is a traditional head covering." She thought about the chalices he used that looked like communion cups, then added, "Receiving the body and blood of Christ is called the Sacrament of the Eucharist, and we're supposed to be without sin and in a state of grace to receive it."

"I know what the Eucharist is." He turned toward her. "But no one is without sin, Emily."

She responded quickly, "Catholics go to confession, but we have to be truly sorry for our sins."

"Have you been confessing your affair with me?"

How could she confess something that she continued to repeat, that she couldn't find the will to resist? "I've been praying that this doesn't turn out badly."

"I've never prayed, but I've heard Marcus and Jake pray. When the demon was conjured and it unleashed its fury, they begged God for someone to save them."

Emily stared at him. Was he the boy the creature had found most susceptible? The one who *hadn't* asked God for help?

He returned to the pictures. "Are these your parents? They look like nice people."

His abrupt change of topic wrenched her heart. "They were. I loved them very much."

"Marcus loved his parents, too. Did Jane tell you that he mentioned them to her?"

"Yes, she did." Emily's heart wrenched a little tighter. Her parents had been killed in a car accident and Marcus's had been victims of a carjacking. "You've never spoken about your family, Damien."

"Marcus and Jake are my family."

She was talking about his birth family, but he'd evaded the reference. For all she knew, his childhood was worse than Jake's or Suzanne's. Was that why he'd never learned to pray?

"Should we go now?" he asked.

She'd almost forgotten about their outing. But she cleared her thoughts, and they left the house.

The craft fair was being held at the same park in her neighborhood where she and Damien had shared the picnic bench and where he'd told her the details about the magic spells.

Details that she no longer believed were accurate.

As they strolled along the grassy aisles, they wandered in and out of booths. The crafts included jewelry, candles, woodwork, and bath and body products.

When they came across a vendor who sold paper goods, Emily noticed a greeting card collection that depicted angels.

Some were cherubs and some were archangels. But the card that caught her attention had a guardian on it. He had a youthful presence, like a teenage boy, but stronger. He was tall and muscular with enormous wings and a plate of armor. In his hand, he carried a steel sword.

Mesmerized, she reached for the card. "Look, Damien, this is the type of angel you and your friends tried to summon." She remembered him describing a similar image. Still fixated, she examined it closer. Although the warrior was enveloped in a cloudy white mist and his features were barely visible, he had wavy dark hair, remarkably similar to Damien's. "He actually looks like a younger version of you."

"He does not."

She held it toward him. "Yes, he does."

She glanced up and saw that he'd taken a step back, away from her, away from the guardian.

"I'm not an angel," he said. "Nor have I ever been one."

She snapped out of her trance. "I didn't say you were." A celestial being wouldn't be masquerading as a demon, and no matter how beautiful Damien was or how angelic his appearance was, she knew better than to think he was from heaven.

Nonetheless, she challenged him. "If angels disturb you so much, why did you participate in trying to summon one?"

"They don't disturb me. I just don't think it looks like me."

Yes, it did. And the more she thought about it, the more it troubled her. He'd never even said a prayer, yet he resembled a servant of God. Then again, it wasn't a real guardian and wasn't as if Damien had painted it. Surely he would have admitted if it was some sort of twisted self-portrait. She turned it over just to be sure.

"You're not going to buy that, are you?"

"No." She returned the card to its rack. He wasn't the artist.

The rest of their date continued in an awkward vein, and by the time they returned to her apartment, her emotional shape worsened.

Damien spoke upon entering the door. "I'm sorry, Emily."

"For what?"

"Spoiling your day."

"It wasn't your fault. It's just something that happened."

Offering comfort, he wrapped her in his arms, and the warmth of his body made everything seem all right, even if she knew it wasn't. She should end their affair. She should send him far, far away. But she did the opposite and led him to her room.

Sex wasn't supposed to be part of the equation, at least not today, but she couldn't seem to stop herself from wanting him.

"Why do you keep doing this to me?" she asked.

"Doing what?"

"Tempting me."

He produced a condom from his pocket. "Maybe it's you who is tempting me."

Was she too mixed up to know the difference?

He peeled his T-shirt over his head, and she followed suit

and unbuttoned her blouse. One by one, they removed articles of their clothing and discarded them.

Naked and aroused, he eased her onto the bed and roamed her flesh as if he were mapping it. Every touch was fresh and new and beautifully frightening. If she'd been falling in love with him before, she was in serious trouble now.

He used the condom, but sheathing his penis wasn't enough. Emily needed protection from his aura.

Daylight illuminated the room, and as he entered her, a warm glow surrounded him. It created a halo-type effect.

Making him look even more like the angel he wasn't.

Fifteen

As Suzanne unloaded the groceries she'd brought to Jake's house, he scowled. He obviously wasn't keen on the idea of her fixing dinner for him.

But she was doing her darnedest to make it a positive experience. She wanted Jake to feel closer to her. At this point, she'd decided not to obsess about who the demon was.

Honestly, what was so bad about it? If she and her friends had been troubled teens alone on the streets and one of them had become inhabited by a dark spirit, they would've stuck by each other, too. And now she was sticking by Jake, no matter what his part in the possession was.

He gave the groceries another displeased look. "I normally eat out."

"I figured you did. That's why I brought some of my own cookware." Just in case he didn't have the required pieces.

"What's with these?" He lifted the mustard greens.

"They're loaded with vitamins."

"Oh, joy."

She refused to let his sour attitude stop her. "Don't get your boxers in a wad. I found a southern-style recipe online that looks really yummy."

"My boxers in a wad? You know darn well that I go commando. And what's this southern stuff? Just because I'm from Georgia doesn't mean I eat greens."

"You're going to learn to eat them."

"They'd better not suck."

She ignored his complaint. "We're going to have fried ham and sweet potatoes, too. Oh, and corn bread."

He relented. "That's starting to sound good."

She smiled to herself for winning the battle, and as soon as the groceries were unpacked, she got the meal under way.

While she worked, he hung around and watched, and after the corn bread was in the oven, he leaned over her shoulder and sniffed the air.

"I would have given my left nut to have my mom cook for me when I was a kid," he said.

Suzanne turned to face him. She wanted to touch his cheek, or skim his jaw or to do something tender, but he'd just skewered a piece of ham from the skillet and was stuffing it into his mouth.

"What about your right nut?" she joked.

"That one, too." He finished eating the stolen ham. "I have a confession to make."

"You actually like mustard greens?"

"No. But I probably will after you season them. My confession is about the other night at the club." He leaned against the counter. "I know who was behind the mirror."

She nearly knocked a spoon onto the floor, making it spin before she caught it. "Who was it?"

"Maybe I shouldn't tell you."

"Jake."

"Okay. It was no one. When I reserved the room, I requested that the viewing room be locked."

"Why?"

"Because I wanted it to be private without you knowing it. That was exciting for me. To keep you to myself when you thought other people were watching."

She thought about how nervous she'd been that night and how deeply the experience had affected her. "I should be mad."

"But you're not?"

"No." The secret intimacy intrigued her. "I like that you wanted to be alone with me."

To show him how much she liked it, she cupped the back of his head and brought his mouth down to hers. He tasted like the honey glaze she'd drizzled on the ham. It was strange for a man's lips to be that sweet. Strange and arousing. She tugged him closer.

They kissed until the timer on the oven went off, jarring them apart and making them smile. The corn bread was ready.

She completed the meal, and they sat down to eat.

He moaned in male appreciation. "You know what, Susie Q? You're a damn fine Suzy Homemaker."

She beamed. "Thank you." He couldn't have said anything that would have pleased her more.

After dinner, he helped her with the dishes, creating a wonderful sense of togetherness and making Suzanne feel as if she belonged in his home.

Later, they shared the couch in the living room. Enjoying the coziness they'd created, she glanced at the bookcase. Then, unable to contain her emotions, she blurted the first thing that popped into her mind. "Maybe your song went magical because you're attached to me, too."

His expression turned hard. "What do you mean 'too'? You said that you weren't having feelings for me."

She couldn't think beyond the clenching of his jaw. Or the pounding of her pulse. "I've been trying to fight it."

"Not very hard, apparently."

"I can't help it." She opened up to him, wanting so desperately for him to care about her in the way she cared about him. "It doesn't even matter to me if you're the demon."

"Don't even go there. Those rumors are bullshit."

"No, they're not. Emily got a 'feeling' that the demon's spirit entered one of you, and then later that day, the masked groom in Damien's painting came alive and looked at her, confirming her suspicion."

He rebuffed the information. "I have no idea what's going on with Damien's work or what Emily's 'feeling' means, but hear me when I say this: the demon is dead."

"Really, Jake, it's okay if the entity is inside you or if you're protecting one of your friends. It doesn't change how I feel."

"You don't know what you're talking about."

"I know what's in my heart." She released a breath that actually hurt her lungs, unable to suppress what was happening to her. "I didn't mean to get attached, but I think I'm falling in love with you."

He flinched, and the air between them turned unbearably thick.

"Say something," she implored him. "Tell me it's all right."

He stood up and moved to the other side of the couch, putting the coffee table between them. He didn't have anything to say, except, "Go home, Suzanne."

"Don't send me away. Please, not now."

"Go home," he ground out again. "And take those damned leftovers with you. I knew I should have never let you cook for me. I should have never hooked up with you to begin with. I can't do this." He moved even farther away from her. "I don't want to do this."

She bit back tears. Not only had she lost Jake, she'd blabbed about the painting. She'd made an absolute mess out of everything. But crying in front of him would only make things worse.

She went into the kitchen and packed her cookware and the food he'd rejected. After she was done, she walked out his door, with no remnants of her having been there.

Except the attachment he refused to feel.

Jane didn't know what to do to make Suzanne feel better. She sat on Jane's sofa, looking like a zombie.

Emily stood beside the window, with her arms wrapped around her middle. Jane didn't know how to comfort her, either.

"I'm sorry." Suzanne spoke to Emily. "I didn't mean to mention the painting."

The brunette turned toward her. "It's okay. I understand that you got caught up in the moment. Besides, it doesn't change anything for me. I know Damien is the demon. I've known from the beginning that it's him."

Suzanne disagreed. "That's just your fear talking."

"It's more than that. It's the way he looks at me, the way he touches me, the way I'm drawn to him even though I know that being with him puts my soul in jeopardy." She moved away from the window. "I even came across a greeting card that had an angel on it that looked like him."

Perplexed, Jane asked, "A fallen angel?"

"No. A guardian, like the kind they tried to summon. Damien got defensive when I questioned him about it."

Still baffled, Jane cocked her head. "Wouldn't his resemblance to a guardian make him seem like less of a demon to you?"

"It would have, I suppose, if he had a religious side. But Damien has never even prayed."

After Emily repeated the details, including how Jake and Marcus had prayed for someone to save them while the demon they'd conjured was unleashing its fury, Jane wondered if Emily was right. Clearly, Damien's lack of faith could have left him open to a possession.

Emily reiterated, "It's him. I just know it."

Suzanne heaved a saddened sigh. "All I can feel is Jake's rejection."

Jane thought about her own feelings for Marcus. She'd finished the article last night and had emailed it to her editor this morning. But she hadn't mentioned the gossip at the club. She'd become too close to Marcus to bring it to public attention.

Did that mean she was falling in love, too? That beneath the banner of submissive sex, she'd discovered something deeper?

"What do we do now?" Emily asked.

Jane considered the question. Banding together and threatening to break up with the men was no longer an option. Jake had already broken up with Suzanne, and Emily looked too fragile to do anything.

"I'll talk to Marcus," Jane said, knowing it was the only thing left to do. "I'll get the truth out him if it kills me."

The following evening, Jane asked Marcus to meet her at the beach, and they strolled past the shops that lined the boardwalk, sipping gourmet coffee from paper cups.

He'd paired his dom boots with a leather jacket, but since the ocean air was cool and breezy, he didn't look out of place. Jane was warmly attired, too, with jeans and a hoodie.

Just as she planned to start grilling him, he said, "I like coming to the beach at night. Have you ever gone grunion watching?"

She shook her head.

"It's fascinating—the way they appear with the tide, all glittery in the moonlight, and then disappear just as quickly."

"Almost like magic?" she prodded.

He didn't take the bait. "It's just the spawning habits of a strange little fish."

Jane frowned. She hadn't arranged this meeting to discuss grunion runs, and he damn well knew it. "Did Jake tell you that he isn't seeing Suzanne anymore?"

"Yes."

"Did he mention Damien's painting, too?"

"Of course he did."

"Then I assume he told you what our theory about the demon is?"

Marcus didn't respond, leaving the issue unresolved.

They continued walking, and she sipped her coffee. The hot beverage warmed her insides, but at the same time, the caffeine burned her stomach.

When they came across an empty bench that faced the ocean, they headed toward it and sat down. Jane noticed that the building behind them was a tattoo shop.

She glanced over her shoulder and checked out the designs decorating the window. A lot of them were dark in nature, like skulls, snakes, and daggers with blood dripping from the blades. There were boatloads of demons, too, creatures with flesh-eating fangs, angry eyes, spiked wings, and ram-shaped horns.

She turned back and caught Marcus watching her.

Silent, he got up and walked over to a trash can to discard his empty coffee cup. In spite of the acid burn, she kept sipping hers. She needed the warmth it provided.

When he resumed his seat, she said, "Emily is convinced that Damien is the demon."

He remained mum.

She frowned at him. "I promised I'd find out the truth from you."

He still didn't speak.

She refused to give up. "We were going to form a united front and threaten to break up with all of you if you didn't reveal who it was. But then Jake ended it with Suzanne and put a chink in our plan."

That got his attention. "Why would you think a threat like that would work?"

"Because of the fate issue. If you think each couple is meant to be together, then . . ."

He snared her gaze. "That sounds as if you think the destiny I spoke of involves love."

"Suzanne is in love with Jake."

"And how does Emily feel about Damien?"

"I think she's in love with him, too."

He didn't question her further, and her heart hit her rib cage. He didn't ask her how she felt about him. But she sensed it was on his mind. Too anxious to fuss with her drink, she set the cup on the ground.

Finally, he said, "The fate I spoke of does involve love. I've wanted you since the beginning. As more than my sub." He placed his hand on her knee. "You want that, too, don't you?"

Heaven help her. There was no point in denying it, not to either of them. She nodded, quite shakily, and he stared at her for what seemed like a beautiful amount of time.

Then he said, "I need you to do something for me."

"What is it?"

"Tell Suzanne and Emily that I'm the demon."

Stunned, she sucked in the sea air. "Are you?"

"No."

She gaped at him. "You're not the demon, but you want me to lie to my friends and say that you are?"

"Yes."

"Why would I do something like that?"

"To keep Emily and Damien together, and to give Jake and Suzanne a chance to reunite. If Emily thinks Damien is mortal, she'll quit freaking out about him, and if Jake can quit worrying about all of this and let me shoulder the burden, he might be able to accept how Suzanne feels about him."

Now she was confused. "Why? Is Jake the demon?"

"That part isn't important."

Not important? "I can't lie to my friends, Marcus."

"I'm asking you to protect everyone's fates."

"No, you're not." As much as it pained her, she pushed his hand off of her knee. "You want me to dupe my friends so you can protect your brotherhood. Just say it. Name the demon and let me be honest with my friends."

"I'm not going to tell you."

"Then I'm not going to stay with you."

"Don't do this, Jane."

Her heart twisted in her chest. "Tell me or I'm leaving."

"Why can't you just let it go?"

"Why can't you just say it?"

"Don't ask me to choose between you and my brothers."

The twisting got tighter. "Because you'll choose them?"

"No, Lady Jane, because I'm afraid I'll choose you."

Sixteen

He couldn't have said anything that would have surprised her more. Or made her more suspicious. What proof did she have that his feelings for her were real? That he wasn't playing a game?

"Tell me who it is," she said.

He didn't respond.

Damn him. She stood up, and before she shattered into a zillion little pieces, she walked away.

But she didn't get far.

He said from behind her, "It's who you think it is."

She spun around, her legs going rubbery. "I never said who I thought it was."

"No, but you agree with Emily, don't you?"

She returned to him. "That it's Damien? Tell me for sure. Say it without masking it."

He blew out a ragged breath. "It's Damien."

Lord Almighty. He'd just chosen her over the boys he'd been protecting since he was a teenager.

She reached for his hand and squeezed it. "Thank you."

He laughed a little brokenly. "I can't believe I just did that."

Neither could she. She held fast to his hand. "Will you tell me all of it now? Will you tell me how Damien became a demon?"

"Yes, but he didn't become one. That's what he has always been. Jake and I didn't meet him on the streets. Damien appeared during the spell."

Holy mother. "He's the creature you conjured? You guys kept saying it was dead."

"He isn't that creature. He's a different one. The first thing that appeared was horrendous. A wrath demon from an infernal legion in hell. But that's what we were trying to conjure."

"Why did you choose such a horrendous thing?"

"Because we thought it was going to be our ally, and we wanted a really bad-ass creature on our side."

Jane glanced at the demons plastered on the glass. "Did it look like any of those?"

He pointed to a monstrosity with scaly skin, gnarled features, piercing yellow eyes, and enormous bat-shaped wings. "This would be the closest depiction. But worse."

She couldn't help but shiver.

"It swooped out of the air and blasted us," he said. "Its energy was everywhere. But mostly it was inside us, clawing at our souls. It was the most immense pain imaginable, like being on fire and having your guts pulled out and your flesh torn off at the same time. We were screaming like crazy, but we were in an abandoned warehouse and there was no one around to hear us."

"Oh, Marcus."

"It was even more painful for Jake because he didn't know how to control his thoughts the way I did. I've always had a strong mind."

He took an audible breath, and she sat quietly, waiting for him to resume the story.

He continued, "I started to pray, and I reached for Jake's hand, too. He summoned the willpower to join me, and we prayed together. Then we chanted the words to the old angel spell that had failed, and that's when Damien showed up. That's how we conjured him."

"How does the angel on the card Emily saw fit into this?" With the direction of how his story was headed, she knew it was too significant not to be part of it.

"That painting was in a book we'd seen at the magic shop where we got our supplies. It's how we imagined a guardian. It's the image that was in our heads during the first angel spell, and we automatically imagined it again when we were chanting and praying this time. Only Damien isn't an angel. He's a demon that descends from fallen guardians. So when he appeared, he looked like a hybrid of the painting. He didn't have the armor or the sword, and although his wings were white, they were tipped in black."

"So Damien got caught in the vortex of your imaginations and his real appearance merged with the image on the card?"

"Yes, but there's another detail about him that I need to mention. His eyes were as red as hot pokers." Marcus made a face. "They still are."

Oh, Lord. "What about your eyes? And Jake's? Are they damaged or is protecting Damien's identity the real reason you wear contacts?"

"Our eyes are fine. We do it for him. But when we first saw him, we didn't know what he was. Good, evil, or something in between. At that point, I don't think he knew, either. He hesitated for a second, then he attacked the other creature. When they were battling, Damien's energy entered us. He was trying to stop the other demon from torturing us. We could feel the push-pull between them, and eventually Damien killed it."

"How?"

"Toward the end of the battle, the sword from the painting appeared and came swirling into the room. It landed in the corner and imbedded itself into the ground."

Jane got a mental image of something similar to Excalibur.

"Damien wasn't able to reach it at first, but he finally managed to grab it and pull it out of the ground. He rammed it through the other demon's chest, and after the creature disintegrated, Damien stepped back and dropped the weapon. Those types of swords are extremely powerful and are only meant to be used by guardians. The aftereffect made him dizzy and he stumbled to the floor."

Riveted to the story, she asked, "What happened next?"

"As soon as the dizziness passed, the sword disappeared, right along with his wings. But his eyes never changed. Proof, he says, that he's a demon and not a guardian. But either way, handling the sword and using it to save us made it impossible for him to return to his realm, so he remained with us and we left Chicago and traveled around together."

"Chicago?"

"That's where the warehouse was. That's where Jake and I were at the time. Later, we all came to L.A. and worked on our careers. Damien is immortal, but he is able to make himself look as if he's getting older. In some ways, he can mimic us, and in other ways, he can't."

"Like turning his eyes into a normal color?"

Marcus nodded.

"What kind of demon is he?"

"He's a carnal entity. They feed off of erotic energy and tempt people to do erotic things. His guardian ancestors were tempted by illicit behavior, and that's how they became demons."

"Is that's why you and Jake are so sexual, from being around Damien?"

"When his energy was inside us, we became part of him. So,

yeah, being attached to him nourishes our fantasies and makes us hungry to act on them. But sharing the same energy is also how we're able to block other supernaturals from knowing who the real demon is."

"And now I have to tell Emily."

"I wish you wouldn't."

"I know, but she has the right to hear the truth." Curious, she asked, "How did he get the name Damien?"

"Jake and I chose it. We were going to call him Gabriel, after the archangel, but since he kept insisting that he was a demon, we called him Damien."

She frowned. "Like the boy in *The Omen*?"

"It was the only demon name we could think of."

Damn. Auntie Em was right about the origin.

Marcus said, "You can see now why Jake and I changed our last names. We didn't want anyone tracing our roots and discovering that we had a past and Damien didn't."

"What's he going to say when he finds out that you told me and that I'm going to tell Emily?"

"Considering the circumstances, I'm sure he'll understand. He wouldn't want me to lose you over this."

She gazed at him, grateful that he was human and guilty that he wasn't. "Do you think fate will intervene? Do you think it's possible for everything to turn out all right?"

"For the others? I don't know. But it's working for us." He reached for her. "I love you, Jane."

"I love you, too," she whispered, holding on to him as if they were the only two people on earth.

Emily should have been prepared. She'd feared all along that Damien was the one. Deep down, she'd known it was him. But hearing the details sent her into a tailspin.

Jane had just told her everything. Suzanne was there, too. The three of them sat on Emily's patio. Her favorite spot with her cute little herb garden, and now the potted plants seemed to be mocking her.

She glanced at the oregano. She remembered Damien telling her that it was once used as protection from demons. But nothing had protected her from developing heart-crushing feelings for him.

By now, Jane had turned quiet, and Emily assumed that she felt terrible for being the bearer of god-awful news. But Suzanne wanted to discuss it, and she engaged Emily in a conversation.

"I think he's a good match for you," the blonde said.

Emily stared at her. "How do you figure?"

"He's almost an angel."

"Descending from fallen guardians doesn't make him an angel." Emily thought about him having red eyes and shuddered. Those eyes were the gateway to his soul. "He has angelic qualities because Marcus and Jake imagined him that way. But even their imaginations couldn't make everything about him beautiful. His real appearance could be as frightening as one of the creatures in his paintings."

"At least give him credit for killing the other demon. When Marcus and Jake needed someone to save them, Damien behaved like a guardian. If it was me, I'd keep seeing him. I'd try to nurture the good in him."

"I'm not a miracle worker. I can't change what he is. And if I stay with him, it would be like denouncing my faith. Everything I feared has come true. Even his name stems from a demonic source."

Jane finally interjected. "Would it have made a difference if they'd called him Gabriel?"

"No," she admitted. He would still be a demon.

Suzanne spoke again. "Are you going to at least talk to him?"

"And say what?"

"You can ask him why he saved Marcus and Jake. You can discuss his true appearance instead of speculating about it. You can question him about how he feels inside. There are lots of things you can talk to him about."

"You make it sound so easy. But I'm afraid of getting close to him. Every time I see him, I want to be with him, and I can't be with him now." Not after she absolutely, positively knew the truth.

Suzanne said, "I think him feeding off of erotic energy is sexy."

"Of course it's sexy. That's why he's so tempting. That's what his purpose is. He's dangerous, especially to someone like me."

Suzanne frowned. "Your rejection is probably going to devastate him."

"I just can't bring myself to see him. He's still a demon, and he's still my worst sin. I should have never started having an affair with him in the first place."

"But you love him, don't you?"

Her stomach clenched. "Yes." She was terribly, achingly in love with him. "But now it's time for me to go to confession and receive my penance." She couldn't even imagine how many rosaries she was going to have to recite.

Suzanne defended her opinion. "Granted, I'm not the overly religious type. But I believe in a higher power, and in my opinion turning your back on him is an even bigger sin."

If only Emily felt that way.

"But you know what this has taught me?" Suzanne went philosophical. "To not give up on the one I love. I'm going to go to Jake's house tonight and try to make things right between us. I think all of them are amazing men, and we should do whatever we can to keep them in our lives."

"Damien isn't a man," Emily reminded her, and she was going to stay as far away from him as she could.

No matter how much she missed him.

Seventeen

Jake wasn't home, so Suzanne headed to the club to see if he was there. She approached the front desk. The blonde receptionist, the Eye Candy girl, was behind the counter.

Suzanne asked, "Do you know if Jake Keller is around?"

The other woman smiled. "Sure, he's here."

"Then I'd like to go in, too."

"Okay. I just need to see your pass."

"I don't have one." She'd borrowed Jane's membership keycard to enter the parking lot, but it was ineffective now that she was in the lobby. Still, she used what little clout she had. "You've seen me here before, with Jake and with my friend Jane. She interviewed you for her article."

"I know who you are. But you still need a pass."

Damn. On the occasions she was with Jake, he'd prearranged for her admittance, and on her first visit to the club, Jane had scored the passes ahead of time. "Can't you budge, just this once?"

"Oh, I'm sorry, I can't."

Double damn. "Is there anyone who can get me in on the spot?"

"Noah can grant you entrance."

Suzanne had yet to meet the owner, but she didn't see any reason for him to deny her. "Would you mind calling him and asking if it's okay?"

"Sure, that's fine."

Candy reached her boss on the phone, but he didn't readily agree. He wanted to talk to Suzanne first, so she took a seat and waited for him. She blew out an antsy breath. All she wanted to do was try to reconcile with Jake, but this place was starting to feel like Fort freaking Knox.

Noah showed up about ten minutes later, but he didn't look like the mountain lion Jane had described. He was simply a tall, insanely handsome man with amazing cheekbones, a rangy build, and long, sleek black hair. But she didn't let his human appearance fool her. She didn't doubt that he was a shapeshifter and that he'd founded the club as a supernatural playground.

He sat next to her. "Hello, Suzanne."

"Hi." In spite of her anxious mood, she smiled, hoping to stay on his good side.

He scanned the length of her. "It's my understanding that you'd like a pass."

"Yes."

"Because you want to see Jake?"

"Yes."

"Why didn't he arrange to have you here as his guest?"

Well, hell. "He broke up with me."

"I see." Noah frowned. "You're not going to hassle him, are you? I don't want any trouble at my club."

Suzanne sighed. She hadn't intended to explain her personal business, but what choice did she have? "I came here to try to make things right between us."

Noah cocked his head. "With sex?"

"With love. But I promise I won't cause a scene."

"Even if he's with another groupie?"

She hadn't considered Jake being with someone else, and the very idea made her queasy, turning her already-nervous stomach on end. "If that's the case, I'll walk away." She paused to reconsider. "Not forever. But for now."

"All right. But for the record, he's by himself. The last I saw of him, he was hanging out on the second floor and looking downright miserable."

"Thank you for letting me know."

"You're welcome. But don't tell him that I ratted him out. I'm supposed to be one of the bad guys."

In some ways, Noah still seemed like a bad guy.

He signed his name on a pass and handed it to her. He didn't say good-bye. He got up and reentered the club without glancing back.

Suzanne took a minute to clear her head. No matter how miserable Jake seemed, her victory was far from guaranteed. He'd still ended his relationship with her.

Pulling herself together, she went inside, and amid the noise and music, she proceeded to the second floor.

She spotted Jake in a public viewing section, where groups of people stood in front of glass partitions, watching various types of sexual activity. But he didn't seem all that interested in whatever he was watching. He kept glancing away.

Suzanne headed in his direction, and during one of his distracted glances, he noticed her. Like something out of a movie, they stared at each other from across the room.

They met in the middle.

"What are you doing here, Susie Q?"

Hearing him say her nickname in such a soft and uncertain voice made her want to touch him. But she refrained. "I wanted to see you."

"Why?"

"So we can talk."

He stuffed his hands in his pockets, as if he was fighting the urge to touch her, too. "You already tried to talk to me on the night I sent you away."

"I know, but that was before Marcus confided in Jane, and

before I gave Emily advice about what she should do about Damien."

"We can't discuss any of that here."

"Then let's go someplace where we can be alone."

He agreed, and they left the club and went out to the parking lot, where they sat in Jake's car. He got behind the wheel, and she scooted into the passenger seat.

Now that she had his attention, she hardly knew where to start. He turned to look at her, and she envisioned him as the boy he once was, being ripped apart by a wrath demon.

"I'm sorry for what you had to endure," she said.

"It was our own stupid faults, conjuring a creature like that. We had no business messing with the occult."

"I can't imagine being tortured like that."

"I couldn't fight it the way Marcus was doing. All I wanted to do was die. It took every ounce of strength I had to pray with him, let alone chant the angel spell." He tugged a hand through his spiky hair. "When Damien first appeared, I thought we really had summoned an angel. But then I saw his eyes and those black-tipped wings, and I wanted to die all over again."

"But he saved you."

"He risked his life to protect ours. The other demon could have just as easily destroyed him. After it was over, I sat and cried. Like a big dumb-ass baby."

"I would have cried, too."

"Yeah, but you're a girl."

"Boys are allowed to cry, too."

"Not according to my mom. I wasn't allowed to cry when I was little." He frowned. "She always made me feel like such a screw up."

"But you're not."

"Sometimes I still feel like it. We spent all these years protecting Damien's identity, then my song acts up in front of you and our secret goes up in smoke."

"Your song might have started all of this, but it was Damien's painting that solidified Emily's 'feeling' that the rumor was true."

"He didn't make the painting move."

"And you didn't make the song turn to magic. It was just something that was meant to happen."

His voice turned shaky. "You're right about me being attached to you. I feel it, way down deep, and it scares me."

"I understand." God, did she ever. "It made me feel that way in the beginning, too. But I'm willing to wait for you to get comfortable with it. I won't push you until you're ready."

"It's all so weird." He gazed out the windshield at the cement wall in front of them. "I never expected to get this close to anyone."

She went quiet, as well, digesting their conversation.

He broke the silence. "What advice did you give Emily about Damien?"

"I told her to nurture the good in him, the side of himself he won't accept. But she said that she can't see him anymore. That it would be a sin."

"When he was battling the other demon, I could feel the difference in their energies. The other creature's was hard and cold, and Damien's was light and warm. During that time, he was a guardian, even if he refuses to accept it."

"What's his energy like now?"

"It's wild and thrilling. But it's strong and protective, too. He would save our lives all over again if he had to, and we'd do the same for him. But no one has threatened any of us, at least not physically. I can't say the same for our hearts." He furrowed his brow. "They used to be safe until you and your friends came along."

"And now Emily is turning away from Damien."

"He's a demon, but he'd never hurt anyone. All he does is tempt people to do salacious things." Jake put his hand on her thigh. "Actually, I think he's tempting me right now."

"That isn't funny." But she laughed just the same.

"I'm serious, Suzanne."

She stopped laughing. "You want to mess around? Here?"

"What could be hotter than the parking lot at a supernatural sex club?"

At the moment, she couldn't think of anything better. She peeled off her panties and climbed over the center console to straddle his lap. He kissed her, and she hiked up her dress and grinded against his fly.

"I've never done it in a car before," she said.

"I have. But not in the front seat. This is crazy."

Totally. She was wedged between him and the steering wheel. "Just don't push me against the horn."

He maneuvered his way around her, then opened his zipper and yanked his shirt out of the waistband of his pants. As soon as he shoved them down, his cock sprang free.

He leaned over to get the protection from the glove compartment, only he ended up spilling the box. Condoms flew everywhere. He grabbed the first one that came into reach and opened it with his teeth. Thoroughly aroused, she watched him put it on.

He circled her waist and thrust forward, impaling her hard and quick. They keened out a mutual moan and kissed with teeth-jarring vigor. He bounced her up and down, and she hit her head on the ceiling of the car. But Suzanne didn't mind a few bumps or bruises. Fanatical as the sex was, she was sealing her fate with the man she loved.

With the sun rising in the sky, Emily knelt in front of a trio of graves. Her parents were buried next to each other, and beside her mother was her grandmother.

She placed fresh-cut flowers on each marker. It was the only type of ornament the park allowed, which was just as well, considering how modest her family had been. Their headstones were simple, unlike some of the markers that surrounded them.

She glanced over her shoulder, where a row of garden statues decorated the grounds. Most of them were angels. She'd noticed them in the past and always thought they were pretty, but today, they seemed to be hovering, and their vigilance made her uneasy. A week had passed since she'd learned the truth about Damien, and she'd barely been sleeping or eating, let alone breathing without a pang in her lungs.

She turned back to her family's graves. She'd come here to seek solace, but being in the presence of the dead wasn't helping, and especially not with those meddling angels standing guard. She wished that they would stop looking at her. She wished that she could stop thinking about Damien, too.

Footsteps sounded from behind her, and her heart nearly stampeded its way out of her chest.

Was it Damien? Had he followed her?

She turned slowly, preparing to face him.

But it was Marcus.

He said, "Jane told me where to find you. She's on her way, too. But I understand if you want me to leave."

She took a moment to study him. She hadn't seen him since the night they'd all first met at the club, and he looked different today. Not his appearance. What had changed was his demeanor. He seemed gentler, like he was genuinely concerned about her.

"It's okay if you stay," she told him.

He moved forward and knelt beside her. Then he said, "My parents weren't buried in a cemetery. They were cremated, and their ashes were sprinkled at sea. They'd arranged it themselves. You know, with one of those prepaid plans. But they never got around to making arrangements for what would happen to me if they died."

"I don't know what would have happened to me if my grand-mother hadn't been there to raise me."

He gazed at the headstones. "This is a nice resting spot."

"I always thought so. But now the statues are unnerving me."

"They would probably make Damien shifty, too."

No doubt. She couldn't stop herself from asking, "How is he?"

"He misses you like mad, but he isn't going to call you or show up at your house or try to persuade you to be with him."

"He's letting me go?"

"Not in his mind. You're all he's been thinking about."

"He's all I think about, too, and it's making me sick inside."

Marcus blew out a breath. "When I envisioned you being fated to him, it didn't include you knowing the truth."

"I'm not doing very well with it. I haven't been to confession yet. I haven't done anything except worry about all of this."

"You're in love with a demon. That's a heavy load."

"You have no idea how heavy." She glanced back at the stat-ues. "Has he ever told you why he saved you and Jake? Or how he got caught up in your spell?"

"We questioned him about it soon after it happened, but he didn't want to talk about it."

"And you never brought it up again?"

"There didn't seem to be any point. He became our brother,

and that was that. Demon, angel, or otherwise, we loved him for getting us out of that mess."

"I wish my love for him was that easy."

"Romantic love never is."

"So I learned." She'd been in a fog since she'd first laid eyes on Damien. "Do you know what his real appearance is like?"

Marcus shook his head. "That didn't matter to us. We were too busy dealing with how to mask his eyes and keep his identity a secret. But if you want know those things, you should talk to Damien."

"That's what Suzanne told me I should do."

"Then maybe you should consider seeing him."

"Maybe. I don't know." She was too confused to make a decision.

Marcus glanced at his watch. "What's taking Jane so long?"

Emily managed a halfhearted smile. "She's never been very prompt."

He smiled, too. "Yeah, I noticed that about her."

Finally Jane arrived, with a kiss for Marcus and a hug for Emily. There wasn't much left to say, aside from filling her in on the conversation.

After a short while, their visit ended, and they all got up to leave. Jane and Marcus held hands as they departed, and Emily looped her way around the graves, taking a path that led her away from the angels.

Eighteen

Jane went to Marcus's house, and they fixed lunch and sat at his dining room table.

"I feel guilty that I'm doing so well, and Emily is such a mess," she said.

"Same here about Damien. Only I'm the loudmouth who didn't keep his secret."

"It's better that you didn't. Now that Emily knows the truth, she can make an informed decision, and Damien can stop hiding what he is."

"He's still going to have to hide it from the rest of the world."

Jane tore a piece of the crust off her sandwich. "How many other supernaturals are there at the club?"

"About a hundred, I guess. But I only know who they are because Damien is aware of them and pointed them out."

"Coyote said that he can sense them."

"Coyote? When did you talk to him about this?"

"Oh, I never told you? He showed up one morning at the coffee bar I go to. He warned me about one of you being a real demon. Of course he didn't know which of you it was, but he explained how connected your energy is."

"Did he also tell you that he was hexed by a witch when he was a kid?"

"Yes, but I wasn't sure what to believe." She sat back in her chair. "Why? Was it bullshit? Was he making stuff up? Because if he was, he got the part about you guys right."

"Of course he got it right. Coyote can sense our energy because he's one of the supernaturals."

She blinked. "What?"

"He's a shapeshifter. But he never shifts at the club. Instead, he wears a mask and spins tales about being a human who can detect immortals."

"Oh, my God. That little dweeb is a real coyote?"

"He can't help the games he plays. Being a trickster is part of his nature."

"Well, he certainly tricked me. I would have never guessed that he was real. By the way, he said that there aren't any other demons at the club. Was he bullshitting about that, too?"

"No. That's true. Most demons are too evil for that sort of

environment, and Noah is cautious about attracting entities that would hurt someone."

"Are there any angels?"

He shook his head. "A proper angel wouldn't be hanging around a sex club. Damien is as close as it gets."

"The hybrid you and Jake conjured. Is it any wonder Emily is confused? I honestly don't know what to think of him, either."

Marcus finished his sandwich and opened a bag of chips. "Unlike Suzanne? Who's encouraging Emily to be with him?"

"I'm glad she and Jake worked things out."

"Me, too. You know what, Lady Jane? You ought to move in with me."

His abrupt invitation caught her off guard. "You want me to live here?"

"And marry me, too."

If she hadn't already been sitting down she would have fallen down. He'd just proposed to her?

"I think we're an incredible match, Lady Jane, and we'd have an amazing life together." He searched her gaze. "I can do really hot things to you on our wedding night. Things we haven't done yet. Oh, and we can shop for rings this week. I would have picked one out for you, but I wasn't sure what type of diamond to get." He continued, his voice rife with anticipation, with hope. "We could get married on the beach, maybe within the next few months." He waited a beat. "What do you think?"

She thought he was certifiable, but she was equally nuts. She wanted to love, honor, and *obey* him for the rest of their lives. She wanted everything with Marcus.

"I say, yes. Sir," she added, with a happy quaver in her heart. Overwhelmed, she leaned over to kiss him, to show him how excited she was.

And just like that, Jane was engaged to her master.

While Suzanne prattled about wedding gowns and how she was going to design something spectacular for Jane, Emily's mind drifted to Damien and the frothy cake they'd fed to each other and how it had made her feel like his bride. But it was Marcus and Jane who'd be exchanging vows.

"Are you okay?" Jane asked her.

She snapped to attention. "I'm fine. I'm really happy for you."

"Thank you. It's only been two days since he proposed, but it's going to happen fast." She glanced at Suzanne. "And there's no stopping her."

The blonde grabbed a sketchpad off of her coffee table. "Dang right, there's no stopping me." She drew something quickly and handed it over.

Jane looked at it and laughed, then showed it to Emily. It was a white gown with bondage ties across the front and a veil with a blindfold. Emily laughed, too.

Jane returned the drawing. "I think I'd prefer something a little less conspicuous."

"Spoilsport." Suzanne started on another sketch. "Are we going to be your bridesmaids? Because if we are, I want to design those dresses, too."

"Of course you are. I wouldn't have it any other way. You're like sisters to me."

The way the men were like brothers, Emily thought. She asked Jane, "Have you seen Marcus's real eye color yet?"

"He showed me last night before we went to bed. They're brown."

"What about Jake's?" she asked Suzanne.

"I saw his this morning, and they're blue. But he and Marcus are going to keep wearing their contacts in public. They're going to keep protecting Damien." Suzanne put her sketchpad down. "You really need to talk to Damien, Emily. If you don't, you're not to be able to concentrate on anything else."

"I know." But God, she was scared. "Maybe I should go to his house now. Just do it and get it over with."

"Are you going to call him first?" Jane asked.

She shook her head. "I'd rather not give him time to prepare for me." If she forewarned him, he might plan a seduction, and she needed to protect herself from falling into his bed. All she was going to do was ask him the things that had been weighing on her mind. Nothing more. Nothing less.

A few heartbeats later, Jane and Suzanne walked Emily out to her car, and she promised to call them when it was over. She'd never been this nervous, not even the first time she'd gone to his house.

She arrived with a lump in her throat. She pushed the bell and waited.

He answered the door, and they stood there, staring at each other. His hair was mindlessly messy, and he was wearing jeans streaked with fresh paint. Obviously he'd been working.

"I wasn't expecting company," he said, apologetically. "But I'm glad you're here."

"I'm not going to stay long." That was her way of telling him that she was going to keep her distance, even if she was already dying to run her fingers through his tousled locks.

He invited her inside, and she crossed the threshold into his living room.

"Would you like some iced tea?" he asked. "I made a pitcher this morning."

She accepted his hospitality and followed him to his kitchen.

He poured her a tall glass and garnished it with a lime wheel. She took a sip. The tea was sweetened just right. But everything Damien created was always so perfect.

She wandered over to the sliding glass door that led to his yard. Plants, flowers, and big leafy trees grew in rebellious patterns.

"Would you like to go outside?" he asked.

She nodded. It seemed safer than staying indoors with him, even if his yard looked like the Garden of Eden on a hedonic day. Already clouds were looming.

They picked through the grass and sat on wrought-iron chairs near a protrusion of crimson roses surrounded by a sea of lark-spur. The sound of water bubbled, courtesy of a Roman-style fountain. A nymph danced in the basin, alone in her nakedness and shrouded in beauty.

Struggling to stay focused, Emily turned away from the fountain and gazed at the view, catching glimpses of other homes peeking through the canyon.

Finally, she shifted her attention to Damien. The paint on his pants had dried into vivid shades, adding more color to the garden.

She said, "I have so many questions."

He blew out breath. "Then ask me."

She embarked on the thing that made her the most uncomfortable. "What is your real appearance like?"

He made a full-body gesture. "This is my real appearance. This is how I look now."

"Please don't sugarcoat your answers. You know I was talking about how you looked before."

He remained evasive. "I don't see why it matters."

She put her tea on a side table. "It's just something I need to know."

"So you'll be even more afraid of me?"

"Were you that horrible?"

"You might think so."

"I still need to know."

He spoke in a quiet voice. "All carnal demons are male because the guardians they descended from were males. And like the guardians who came before them, they have pleasant features, human-type bodies and massive wings. Only their wings are black instead of white, and their eyes are red." He frowned. "Their penises are always exposed, too, and the tips are shaped like spears."

Saints preserve her. She recalled his artwork at the club and how uncomfortable it had made her feel. "Like the demon stalking the maiden in the woods?" His penis had been speared, too.

"Yes, but the rest of that creature doesn't resemble a carnal demon. I never paint demons exactly as they are. It's better to fictionalize them. Otherwise, their spirits might be drawn to the paintings."

She warded off a self-imposed chill. "So your identifying features were red eyes, big black wings, and a spear-shaped penis?" She made a face. "If all carnal demons are male, who did you have sex with?"

"I fornicated with female demons from other breeds. But I prefer being with humans. I like that my cock turned smooth, especially since I've been inside you. You make me feel warm, Emily. Warmer than I've ever felt before."

She changed the subject. She couldn't bear to acknowledge his claim or think too deeply about how warm he made her feel. "Tell me how you got pulled into Jake and Marcus's spell. Where were you when it happened?"

"I was at an art museum in Italy, but no one could see me. I was in a state of in-between. My spirit was there, but my physical body was hidden with its own energy. That's how demons can come to earth without being detected."

"Why were you at the museum?"

"I've always been fascinated by man's ability to create art. It's why I became an artist, too. On this particular day I was admiring a portrait of Venus, and then I heard human voices behind me. I turned, but no one was there."

"Where were the voices coming from?"

"A painting of a guardian angel on the wall. It was the original of the image Jake and Marcus had seen in the book in the magic shop. The same image you saw on the card."

Dear God. "You heard Marcus and Jake's prayers through the painting?"

He nodded. "I tried to turn away, but I was compelled to move forward, to their voices, to the painting. The guardian in the picture was depicted as a teenager, which was younger than my physical appearance. But I noticed a resemblance. Our faces were similar, except for our eyes, and our hair was almost the same."

As Emily waited for Damien to finish his story, silence engulfed them. Even the water bubbling from the fountain faded from her ears.

He said, "I sensed that he was an early ancestor of mine, a guardian that hadn't become a demon. I assumed that the artist had painted him from memory. That he must have appeared to her during times of trouble. He should have appeared to Marcus and Jake, too. He should have been the one to help them, but I got mixed up in the spell because I was there, connecting with my ancestor and listening to their prayers. As their chants got louder and louder, I was dragged toward the painting, and I felt my physical being start to change. I was getting younger, my wings were turning white, and my penis was no longer speared. I wasn't naked anymore, either." He paused. "I tried to fight it. I think that's why I didn't change all the way, why my eyes remained red and why the tips of my wings stayed black. I didn't want to become a guardian. I didn't want to be responsible for protecting people or hearing their prayers."

"What happened next?"

"I went through the painting and landed in the warehouse with Marcus and Jake. I simply appeared there."

"And that's when you saw that the other demon was torturing them?"

"I was so confused. I didn't know what I was supposed to do. Wrath demons are stronger than carnal demons. They're big and cruel, with brute muscle and vicious energy. But I couldn't just stand there and watch it tear those boys apart."

So he became a guardian, she thought.

"I didn't have the armor or the sword like my ancestor, but I lunged at the creature anyway, and we engaged in hand-to-hand combat."

She envisioned every detail he was describing.

"I was doing whatever I could to keep the boys alive. I enveloped them in my energy. But I was still losing the battle. I figured we were all going to perish, then I saw that the sword had appeared and was imbedded into the concrete." Memories gathered in words, in the way he clenched his hand. "I struggled to grab hold of it because the other demon kept pulling me away. But eventually I was able to reach it, and as soon as I did, I slammed it into the creature's chest. He exploded and the pieces disintegrated."

"Is that when you got dizzy?"

He nodded. "I dropped the sword and stumbled to the floor. After the vertigo passed, the weapon vanished, my wings disappeared, and I became earthbound. I was forbidden to return to my realm. But I was still a demon."

"You kept telling me you were a man. You kept lying to me."

"I look like a man." He squinted. "Or mostly I do."

"That's not the same as being one."

"If I'd told you the truth, you wouldn't have been with me, and I wanted you more than anything."

"Why do you think your painting came alive in front of me?"

"I think your instincts about me were so strong that the groom was trying to unmask my lies and respond to your fears."

"Only I got some of the details wrong?"

"My lies were well developed."

She questioned him further. "Why do you paint innocent maidens and delicate brides? Do you think it's because you're hungry for someone to tame you?"

He looked into her eyes. "I would let someone tame me if it would make me mortal."

Anxious, she lifted her tea and took a sip. She'd come here for answers, not to help him. But suddenly she wanted to explore the possibility. "Do you love me, Damien?"

He responded without hesitation. "Yes."

She thought about Suzanne's suggestion. She thought about the statues at the cemetery, too, and how they'd been watching her. At the time she hadn't accepted their presence as encouragement, but she should have known better. "Will you let me nurture the good in you?"

His expression turned wary. "That won't turn me into a man."

"What if it does? What if makes the redness in your eyes go away and your soul turn mortal?"

"There's no guarantee that will happen."

"No, there isn't. But if you embrace yourself, the way I'm embracing you, maybe it will."

"Does that mean you love me, too?"

"Yes, very much." He wasn't her greatest sin. He was her greatest love, and he needed her. "But if we're going to be together, you have to want to change."

"What if it never works? Will you still love me then?"

"Yes, I will."

Instead of acknowledging her belief in him, he got up and headed toward the fountain.

Determined to stay close, she followed him.

He turned and asked, "Why would you still love me?"

"Because the good is already inside you. Look at what you did to save Marcus and Jake."

"Yes, but handling the guardian sword made me weak."

She could see how uncertain he was, but she wasn't going to give up. "I'm not asking you to be an angel. I'm just asking you to see the good in yourself. To see what I see."

"I'll try," he replied softly.

"And I'll be here for you. I promise." To prove that she meant it, to show him how much she loved him, she reached out to hold him.

Keeping him close to her heart.

Nineteen

Suzanne had been warning herself not to cry, for all the good it did, and dabbed at her eyes. But at least she'd had the foresight to wear waterproof mascara.

"You look beautiful," she said to Jane. They stood beside each other in a dressing room at a luxurious seaside hotel in Malibu, the lights around the mirror heightening their images.

"It's the dress you designed," the bride responded.

It was more than that. It was the glow of a woman embarking on her future. Of course the dress was pretty remarkable, too, a flowing gown adorned with a jeweled corset and an ebony sash at the waist.

Beach chic with a bit of bondage.

Emily walked up to the mirror, and the three of them

exchanged a smile. Suzanne and Emily sported red dresses with a hint of black tulle.

The ceremony was as at dusk, and the time was growing near.

Marcus wanted an evening wedding so the vampires from the club could attend. Not that the regular guests would know that a nocturnal creature might be sitting next to them. Suzanne still didn't know who the supernaturals were, aside from Noah and Coyote. Jane and Emily didn't know, either. But none of them cared anymore. They had their men. Or their "almost" men. Damien was still a work in progress.

Suzanne reached for the bride's trailing rose bouquet and handed it to her.

"My parents think I've gone Goth," Jane said. "Marrying a hypnotist with black eyes. But they like him anyway."

"What's not to like about a tall, dark, and handsome guy who adores their daughter?"

"And chains her to his bed," Emily quipped from the sidelines.

A knock sounded at the door, and they all jumped to attention.

Jake poked his head inside. "Let's go, Susie Q. You, too, Emily." He grinned at Jane. "Marcus is chomping at the bit to get to you. Oh, and your dad is ready, too. He's waiting to walk you down the beach."

The procession started with Suzanne and Jake, then Emily

and Damien. Everyone shared equal billing. Two bridesmaids and two best men.

It unfolded beautifully, with a sandy aisle that led to a make-shift gazebo, and after the happy couple recited handwritten vows, a reception at the hotel followed.

Later, with the moon waxing the sky and the hum of champagne in their blood, Suzanne and Jake kissed. The reception was winding down, and they were ready to go to their room.

Only Jake guided her toward the tropical foliage in a dimly lit courtyard instead.

"What are you doing?" she asked.

He pressed her against the bark of a towering palm tree. "Ravishing you."

She turned instantly thrilled, instantly nervous, too. The risk that came with getting caught never ceased. Her heart pounded beneath her breastbone.

He nibbled playfully at her neck. "I love how you react to me. I love everything about you."

It was the best thing he could have said, the deepest and most exciting aphrodisiac.

She inhaled the scent of the sea air. She breathed in his cologne, too. "I feel the same way about you."

"I know." He smiled, and his teeth flashed in the dark. "You're my girl."

At this point, they hadn't made any plans for the future. They were still taking "I love you" one day at a time. But being referred to as his girl was monumental, and she cherished the sound of it. She leaned in for a tongue-thrusting kiss and their mouths met in luscious abandonment.

"I'm going to make you come, Susie Q. Right here and now."

"Promise?"

"Yes, ma'am." He bunched the hem on her dress.

She sighed.

He slipped past the elastic on her panties and put his fingers against her ever-swelling clit. Rubbing in tiny circles, he made her hot and wet and eager.

Somewhere in the middle of it, he brought his fingers to his lips and tasted them. She flexed and moaned.

When he got down on his knees, lust exploded beneath the surface of her skin. He took her panties off and told her to hold her dress up.

She gripped the fabric and offered him unlimited access to her body. He licked her labia and kissed her clit, giving her the orgasm of a lifetime, and while Suzanne shook and shuddered, she couldn't think of a better way to share Jane and Marcus's wedding night.

"It was a beautiful wedding," Emily said to Damien, as they entered their hotel room.

"Yes, it was." He turned to admire her. "You look good in red. Your dress is the same color as my eyes."

"That's a bad joke."

He smiled. "Maybe, but it's true." He went into the bathroom to take his contacts out. He'd been making a habit of being himself around her, but they were living together now, sharing his home in the canyon.

He returned, and she gazed unblinkingly at him. She loved him, even with those fiery eyes.

She went over to him and slipped her arms around his waist. "Someday you're going to be mortal." It was a belief they were determined to share.

They went reverently quiet until he said, "I've been thinking about the changes that will occur."

"How so?"

"Regardless of how human I become, it's not going to alter my sexual appetite. That's been ingrained in me for too long."

Being a highly erotic man wasn't the same as being a carnal entity, but she understood what he meant. "I'm okay with that. I love how sensual you are."

He smiled and went over to the nightstand and removed a glass bottle. "It's massage oil." He uncapped it. "Yarrow, peppermint, lavender, lemon balm, and sage."

Emily inhaled the fragrance. "It's wonderful." On the night they'd first made love, they'd talked about using those ingredients to make massage oil. But rose petals were supposed to be part of the mixture, too. Had he forgotten?

No, she realized, he hadn't. The omission had been deliberate.

He unpinned the boutonniere from his lapel, plucked the petals from the flower and dropped them into the bottle.

A rose had never been sweeter.

He led her to bed and stripped off her clothes. He shed his, as well.

With the lights turned low, he proceeded to give her an exquisite massage. With each touch, with each warm caress, she fell deeper in love.

"Someday I want you to marry me," he said.

"Someday" meant when he was mortal. "You know I will." She longed to become his bride.

He continued the massage, roaming his hands over her skin. He circled her breasts, teased her nipples, then trailed a tender path down her stomach and across her mound.

But the sexual spa didn't end there. Afterward, he suggested a bath, so they headed for the tub.

He filled it with warm water and added powdered milk and honey he'd brought from home. He was full of romantic surprises.

As he leaned back, she settled between his legs. He looped his arms around her, and she scooted her bottom deliciously close to his cock.

He stirred from her touch, and soon she was on her hands and knees in the water, Damien preparing to mount her.

With milk and honey sloshing around them, he entered her.

While he rocked back and forth, she swayed in a sea of emotion, her future husband deep inside her.

Jane gazed longingly at her husband. Earlier, he'd tied her to a chair and that was where she remained, waiting for whatever came next.

They were in the honeymoon suite at the hotel, and it was filled with extravagant antiques. Only the chair he'd chosen was simple, a straight-back style from the early 1900s.

What a sight she must have made, still wearing her wedding gown with her arms bound behind her back.

Marcus looked powerful as hell. He'd changed out of his tuxedo, switching to a gauzy white shirt, black breeches, and English equestrian boots.

He removed a riding crop from his luggage and placed it on the four-poster bed. Her pulse fluttered between her legs. Was he going to whip her tonight? Was it actually going to happen?

"You'd better be good, Lady Jane," he said.

"I will." Or as good as the situation allowed. She couldn't help but crave his punishment.

He removed another item from his luggage and held it up for her to see. It was a set of nipple clamps attached to a glittering chain.

"What do you think?" he asked.

It was elegantly depraved. "The jewels are the same as the ones on my dress."

"So they are." He flashed a much-too-dashing smile. "I asked a little bird to make it for me."

Suzanne, she thought.

He said, "She wouldn't give me details about the gown, but she was quite accommodating as far as this was concerned." He dangled the chain. "It was her first BDSM piece, and she promised it would complement your dress."

"Your wedding gift to me?"

He nodded. "And I'm going to put it to good use."

Her pulse fluttered again.

Marcus walked over to her, his strides long and deliberate. He leaned over and unhooked the front of her gown, loosening the corset and exposing her breasts.

"Do you recall the watercolor from the club?" he asked.

Ah, yes. The nipple-clamped girl Damien had painted for Marcus. "She was tied to a chair, too."

"Re-creating it has always been a fantasy of mine, and now I'm making it come true. With my wife."

His wife. If she hadn't been on the verge of being clamped, she would have melted. "How tight are you going to make them?"

"The amount of pressure you feel depends on your sensitivity level. But you can stop me if it's too much. Your safe words still apply."

She wouldn't dream of stopping him, but she played along. "Yes, sir."

He attached the first clamp, and a gust of air escaped her lungs. It pinched like a mother, but it aroused her, too. He attached the second clamp, and in spite of her bonds, she nearly pitched forward.

Twice the ache, twice the thrill.

He removed the black sash from her dress. "This is clever. A wedding gown blindfold. Was it your idea or Suzanne's?"

"It was hers, but I approved it."

He looped it around his neck and tied it like an ascot. "Do you want me to use it on you later?"

At the moment she couldn't think past her aching nipples. The longer the clamps stayed on, the more it hurt.

"Do you?" he asked again.

She jerked out a nod.

"And the whip? Do you want me to use that, too?"

She glanced at the bed, and her voice vibrated. "Yes."

After he removed the clamps, the sensation got worse. She assumed it was her blood rushing to her nipples to revitalize the area. Finally the numbness passed, and he rewarded each breast with a soft kiss, making her tingle all over.

He released the knots on the rope that secured her to the chair. She got up, and he helped her out of her dress, leaving her in a white silk thong and thigh-high stockings trimmed in lace.

"Bridal lingerie," he said, gazing at her with lust in his eyes.

She'd never felt more beautiful. But that was how a woman should feel on her wedding night.

Marcus gazed at her a while longer, then stripped her bare. Once she was naked, he lifted the riding crop and turned down the bed. He ordered her onto the mattress with her butt high in the air.

Although he didn't restrain her, he wrapped the sash around her eyes and tied it. In the darkness, he came up behind her and ran the whip along the crack of her bottom.

As always, he teased her. On and on it went, until she thought she might die.

Finally, he cracked it lightly across her ass, and she reached down to stroke herself.

"You're a bad girl," he said.

Yes, she thought. Very, very bad.

He swatted her again, and she rubbed a little harder. She was too excited not to come.

But Marcus made her stop. Orgasm denial. She cursed him adoringly in her mind.

He used the whip a few more times, and as light as his touch was, she suspected that she had marks just the same.

"You should have been the demon, sir."

"I warned you from the beginning that I was demonic in bed." He removed the blindfold and spun her around and into his arms.

He shoved down his pants and his penis sprang free. A better sight didn't exist. She wanted him so badly, she tore at his shirt. They both went feral, clawing and kissing and rolling over the bed. In the midst of it, his clothes came off, his boots flying across the room.

Jane breathed a sigh of hunger, and Marcus pushed her legs open. Desperate to consummate their vows, they mated like the dom and sub they were.

Newly married and wickedly in love.